"If you'd like me to come in and check..."

"No, no, that won't be necessary," Harriet told Rigg hastily, stepping back so quickly that she slipped off the path and lost her balance.

Rigg reached out immediately to steady her. As though he felt the shock that rippled through Harriet, his fingers fastened around her upper arm, tightening momentarily. The headlights of the Range Rover showed his dark profile bent toward her.

"You're quite safe," he told her curtly. "Despite the impression given to you by my niece as to the dastardliness of my nature, I assure you that my failings do not run to base inclinations."

It ought to have been the easiest thing for her to have reassured him, but for some stupid reason she started to tremble helplessly, and she felt his intent gaze search her face.

PENNY JORDAN was constantly in trouble in school because of her inability to stop daydreaming—especially during French lessons. In her teens she was an avid romance reader, although it didn't occur to her to try writing one herself until she was older. "My first half-dozen attempts ended up ingloriously," she remembers, "but I persevered, and one manuscript was finished." She plucked up the courage to send it to a publisher, convinced her book would be rejected. It wasn't, and the rest is history! Penny is married and lives in Cheshire.

Penny Jordan's striking mainstream novel, *Power Play*, quickly became a *New York Times* bestseller. She followed that success with *Silver*, a story of ambition, passion and intrigue.

Watch for Penny's latest blockbuster, *The Hidden Years*, available in October wherever paperback books are sold.

Books by Penny Jordan

HARLEQUIN PRESENTS
1282—BEYOND COMPARE
1297—FREE SPIRIT
1314—PAYMENT IN LOVE
1324—A REKINDLED PASSION
1339—TIME FOR TRUST
1353—SO CLOSE AND NO CLOSER
1369—BITTER BETRAYAL

HARLEQUIN SIGNATURE EDITION
LOVE'S CHOICES
STRONGER THAN YEARNING

Don't miss any of our special offers. Write to us at the following address for information on our newest releases.

Harlequin Reader Service
P.O. Box 1397, Buffalo, NY 14240
Canadian address: P.O. Box 603,
Fort Erie, Ont. L2A 5X3

PENNY JORDAN

breaking away

Harlequin Books

TORONTO • NEW YORK • LONDON
AMSTERDAM • PARIS • SYDNEY • HAMBURG
STOCKHOLM • ATHENS • TOKYO • MILAN

Harlequin Presents first edition August 1991
ISBN 0-373-11388-9

Original hardcover edition published in 1990
by Mills & Boon Limited

BREAKING AWAY

CHAPTER ONE

HARRIET grimaced to herself as she realised she was not going to make it to the village before dark.

It was her own fault; she had been later leaving London than she had planned, and then she had made that motorway stop mid-afternoon. Already it was dusk, and it would be a good half-hour yet before she reached the village and her new home.

Louise had told her she thought she was mad when she had announced her plans.

'Leave London for a small remote village lost in the Scottish Borders?' She had shuddered, even at the end of the telephone, but then she and her sister had never had similar tastes.

Thinking of her sister made Harriet feel uncomfortable and anxious, a legacy from those early years after their parents' deaths when she had first started to shoulder the burden of her sister's irresponsibility.

There were four years between them, and it had surely only been natural that when their parents died she should have immediately abandoned her own plans for teaching abroad, and instead taken a job in London, so that she could take care of her younger sister and provide a home base for her.

She had been twenty-two then and Louise eighteen. Louise had always been rebellious and self-willed, and when, after a few months, Harriet used her own half of their shared inheritance from their parents' estate to buy a small house, albeit in a then unfashionable area of London, so that she could provide a home for her sister, Louise had announced that she was going to use part of her own inheritance to pay for an expensive modelling course.

Louise was a beautiful girl—Harriet had not been able to deny that—but she had still tried to dissuade her sister, knowing full well that Louise was attracted to modelling because she thought it a glamorous life. Privately Harriet had believed Louise lacked the application and dedication necessary for success in such a very competitive world.

Louise had refused to listen to her. She had flown into a temper and run out of the house, and despite all her attempts to find her Harriet had neither seen nor heard from her for six months. Six months of incredible anxiety and concern, coloured by guilt that she had not handled matters better.

And then, just as she was beginning to pick up the pieces of her own life—just beginning to settle down and find her way in the very large and busy comprehensive where she was teaching English, just beginning to make one or two friends, and to accept dates from a fellow teacher, Paul Thorby—totally out of the blue Louise had returned to announce that she had been living in Italy, modelling there.

There was not a word of contrition for the concern she had caused, or for the anxiety and anguish she had put her sister through; all she could talk about was herself and her own plans, but Harriet was too relieved to chastise her.

She was getting married, she told Harriet, to a wealthy Italian she had met in Turin, adding airily and thoughtlessly that the only real reason she was back in London was to buy her wedding dress.

When Harriet learned that Louise had only known Guido for six weeks, she pleaded with her to wait a little longer, but Louise, as always, refused to listen.

They were married in Turin, two months after they had met, and, while Harriet quite liked her new brother-in-law, she was very uneasy about her sister's ability to adapt to living with her in-laws and the rest of Guido's large family.

Paul Thorby reminded her that Louise was an adult and perfectly capable of making her own decisions. He was a nice man, but pedantic, and inclined to be petulant if he didn't have her full attention. He was an only child, and when he took Harriet home to meet his mother her heart sank as she recognised that she and Sarah Thorby were never likely to get on well.

She was then just twenty-four years old and aware of a vague feeling of dissatisfaction with her life: what had happened to all her bright dreams of travelling or exploring a little of the world, before settling down to her career?

Her parents' deaths had brought a halt to those plans but there was no reason why she shouldn't fulfil them now. Louise was married. She had no one to account to but herself. Perhaps at the end of the school year...

Six months later she was just nerving herself to tell Paul that their relationship was by no means as permanent as he seemed to think, and to explain to him her dreams of being able to travel, when without warning Louise suddenly returned home, announcing that her marriage was over and that she was divorcing Guido.

Dismayed, Harriet tried to persuade her to return to her husband, but Louise was adamant. She found herself a lawyer and instituted divorce proceedings, telling Harriet that she would have to live with her, and when Guido came over to London to see her she shut herself in her bedroom and refused to come out, leaving Harriet to deal with the irate Italian.

From his complaints against his wife, Harriet suspected that Guido had fallen out of love with her sister with the same alacrity with which she had fallen out of love with him. Neither seemed too concerned about the breakdown of their marriage.

Guido returned to Turin, and Louise continued to inhabit the larger of Harriet's two spare rooms.

Paul, who didn't like her, announced to Harriet that she ought to tell her sister to find alternative accommodation, but Harriet was far too soft-hearted and besides Louise wasn't well. She had been sick several times, and she was beginning to look almost haggard... Louise, who had never looked anything less than glowingly beautiful from the moment she was born.

Once, briefly as a teenager, Harriet had envied her younger sister her beauty. Louise took after their paternal grandmother, having thick, pale gold hair, and dark blue eyes, with the kind of complexion that never broke out in spots.

Harriet, on the other hand, took after her mother's side of the family. She wasn't quite as tall as Louise, barely medium height and finely boned.

Her hair was dark, almost but not quite black, with odd red lights in it, so that Paul had once disapprovingly asked her if she dyed it. Her eyes were the only feature she shared with Louise, their density of colour startling against the framework of her pale translucent skin and dark hair.

Harriet had no illusions about herself, aware that she was nowhere near as attractive to men as her sister but with no real wish to be. A natural reticence and shyness had kept her from accepting the overtures made to her during her teenage and university years.

And now there was Paul in her life. If their relationship lacked excitement and passion—and if, deep down in a secret part of her, she deliberately kept it on a non-sexual basis because of some silly, romantic daydreams about being swept off her feet by a man who would arouse within her all the feelings that Paul never did—then she suppressed those feelings, and told herself that such an idealistic emotional commitment was not for her.

She was just wondering how soon she could break the news to Louise that she intended to sell the house and go and travel abroad for an indefinite period of time, when Louise dropped a bombshell of her own. She was pregnant, she told Harriet, and no, she had no intention of cancelling the divorce or even of letting Guido know about her condition.

When Harriet tried to counsel her to think about it, she became so hysterical that her sister gave in. Louise was still living with Harriet and after the birth of the twins made it plain that she intended to go on doing so.

How *could* she turn her out? Her own sister and two small babies besides! Harriet protested when Paul suggested that she ought to tell Louise to leave.

Paul had been furious with her and hadn't spoken to her for almost a fortnight.

When he eventually did, she told him that their relationship, such as it was, was over. Then, in the years that followed, somehow or other there was no time in her life for any relationship other than to her role as the main breadwinner and financial support of her sister and her children.

Louise was as irresponsible a mother as she was a sister; one moment spoiling the twins to death, the next ignoring them. After their birth she never went back to work, although she always seemed to have enough money to buy clothes to go out with the various men who dated her.

Harriet loved the twins, but she had to admit they weren't the easiest of children to deal with. Louise never disciplined them herself and refused to allow others to do so.

Life wasn't easy for Harriet although she never complained. Unlike Louise, who seemed for some obscure reason to blame Harriet for her early marriage and the twins' arrival... Then, just after the twins' ninth birthday, something totally unexpected happened, or rather two totally unexpected things happened.

The first, and the more astonishing as far as Harriet was concerned, was that a publisher accepted the children's book she had submitted to the firm.

For as long as she could remember she had scribbled down her 'stories', but it was an article she had read in a magazine that had encouraged her to spend the long winter evenings working on perfecting the short adventure story she had originally written for the twins.

Now, unbelievably, it was going to be published and she was commissioned to write four more.

The other surprise was an announcement from Louise that she was remarrying, to an American who was taking her and the twins back to California with him.

Harriet had known that Louise was involved in another of her brief affairs, but there had been so many that she had not thought this one any more serious than those which had preceded it. Her sister craved admiration in the way that an addict craved drugs or alcohol, and once the current man in her life failed to provide that admiration in full measure she usually lost interest in him.

This time, though, it seemed that she had at last found a man strong enough to cope.

Harriet attended their quickly arranged marriage in a daze of surprise. She hadn't had time to announce her own good news; Louise had as always been too wrapped up in her own affairs to spare the time to listen.

For nearly ten years Harriet had supported her sister and her children, and now totally unexpectedly she was free of that burden. A burden she had willingly shouldered, partly out of love and partly out of guilt—a guilt that sprang from the belief that she was to blame for Louise's flight from their home and her subsequent too early marriage, and that, had their parents not died, Louise would never have left home. Now that burden was removed from Harriet's shoulders, and she was free!

She had never liked living and working in London, and indeed disliked city life, preferring the country. The Border country between England and Scotland had always drawn her, and the weekend after Louise had left for California with her new husband and the twins, Harriet found herself heading north, to spend a glorious week meandering along the peaceful Border roads, enjoying the first real personal freedom of her life, enjoying time to think about her future—to plan!

The decision to sell her London house and move north was made quickly, too quickly perhaps, but Harriet wasn't going to allow herself to regret it.

She had found the house by accident one golden afternoon when she was driving through the tiny village of Ryedale. A mile or so outside the village she had seen the battered 'For Sale' sign posted beside the road, and had gone to investigate, following the lane that was little more than an overgrown and disused cart track, to find the cottage tucked secretly and securely away behind an enormous overgrown hedge.

She had driven straight back to her hotel and telephoned the agents, and by the end of the week she had committed herself to the purchase of the cottage.

The agent had warned her of its many defects: its loneliness, its lack of mains drainage, its unkempt, overgrown garden, and its need for a complete overhaul of the electrical and plumbing installations, but nothing could put her off. She was in love, and like anyone else in that dangerous state, she refused to admit to any flaws in the appearance of her beloved.

Nevertheless she had a full survey done on the house. Built of stone, small and squat with tiny windows and low-beamed rooms, it was surprisingly free of any structural problems.

The buoyancy of the London property market enabled her to sell her own house immediately for what seemed an enormous sum of money, most of which she intended to invest to bring herself in a small 'security net' income. This would keep her going while she discovered if she could actually earn her living as a writer, or if her first success had been merely a fluke.

Her headmaster, when she had told him her plans, had pursed his lips and frowned, pointing out to her the risks she was taking. Teaching jobs were not easily come by where she was going. She was in line for promotion...

Harriet refused to listen. All her life she had been cautious and careful; all her adult life she had been burdened with the necessity of putting others first.

She was almost thirty-five years old and she had had no real freedom, no real opportunity to express herself as an individual. Now fate had handed her this golden chance; if she refused to take it...but she wasn't going to refuse.

She felt happier than she could ever remember feeling in her life; and yet nervous at the same time.

Via the agent, contractors were employed to put right the defects in the plumbing and wiring; a new kitchen was installed in the cottage; and a new bathroom, plus central heating; and now, as autumn set in, Harriet was driving north to begin her new life.

As a final gesture of defiance, she had bundled up all the neat plain skirts and blouses she had worn for school and given them away; and in a final splurge of madness had gone out and re-equipped herself with jeans and thick woollen sweaters bearing funny motifs and in brilliantly bright colours.

She had discarded the serviceable green Hunter wellingtons suggested by the saleswoman when she explained her new lifestyle, and instead had opted for a pair of bright, shiny red moon boots that matched almost exactly the bright red of her hooded duffel coat. Not for her the sombre and correct green of the county fraternity. From now on she was going to be her own person and not conform to anyone else's ideas.

She smiled a little grimly to herself as she drove north. Surely almost thirty-five was rather old to start rebelling against society? Even if that rebellion was only a very small one... Anyway, remote in her small cottage, she doubted if she would see many people to disapprove of her vivid choice of colours.

Of course, it would be nice to make friends, she admitted wistfully. In London there had never seemed to be the opportunity. The other teachers were either younger than she and intent on having a good time when they weren't at work, or older and involved with their families. Louise had sulked every time she had tried to point out that she had a right to her own free time, and in the end it had proved so difficult to have a life of her own, independent of those of the twins and her sister, that she had given up.

She felt guilty at how little she missed them. Louise had left without making any attempt to suggest that her sister visit them. She only hoped that this time Louise stayed married, Harriet reflected. The cottage only had one large bedroom now, the two smaller rooms having been knocked into one and the third bedroom having been converted into a bathroom.

Yes, she was free for the first time since her parents' death. Free to write...to daydream...to enjoy the countryside...to do all those things she had wanted to do for so long...to...

Her thoughts sheered off abruptly, and she braked instinctively, feeling her small VW protest as it squealed to a halt, only just missing the man who had so unexpectedly emerged from the trees shadowing the road and who was even now bearing down on her.

She reacted instinctively to his totally unexpected appearance as any driver would, braking to avoid him, but now as he came towards her she realised two disturbing things simultaneously.

The first was that she had been very foolish to stop the car in the first place, and the second and even more frightening was that the man appeared to be totally naked, apart from a pair of extremely brief briefs.

As far as she could see in the gathering dusk he was also extremely wet, and extremely angry.

Too late she reached out to lock the car door, but he was already wrenching it open, his voice hard and furious as he said bitingly, 'Trixie, what the

hell do you think you're doing? You've had your
little joke, and now if you wouldn't mind giving
me my clothes——'

Two strong hands reached for her, grasping her
arms unceremoniously. She gasped and tensed, fear
flicking through her, and then almost immediately
the hands were withdrawn and an icy male voice
was apologising curtly.

'I'm sorry. I mistook you for someone else. She
drives the same model and colour car. Trixie, I
could murder you!'

He stopped abruptly, almost visibly forcing back
his anger, his forehead creasing into a frown.

He was a tall man, over six feet and powerfully
built, as Harriet had every opportunity to see, and
probably very good-looking when he wasn't so
angry.

He had dark hair, at present almost plastered to
his skull as though he had just been swimming,
which would explain the moisture dripping from
his skin and his almost nude state—but what man
in his senses would be swimming out here alone in
the dark?

Lost in her own thoughts, Harriet suddenly realised that he was apologising to her, though rather
brusquely, explaining that he had mistaken her for
someone else. Someone else who drove the same
make and colour of car.

She focused on him, uncomfortably aware of her
own heightened colour as her brain made the automatic connections between his unclothed body, and
his reference to believing her to be someone else.
Someone else who was surely his lover, and had

obviously been with him and then driven off leaving him.

Suddenly feeling hot and flustered, she was aware of an odd bleakness inside her, an uncomfortable and unwanted realisation that for her there never had been, and now probably never would be, the kind of interlude that might lead to a passionate quarrel such as had obviously provoked her companion's present ire.

She judged him to be three or four years her senior, despite the hard leanness of his body, and wondered idly what his lover was like ... attractive most certainly, sophisticated. How old? Midtwenties? And then realised that he was asking her if she would give him a lift.

A lifetime of caution screeched loud warning bells in her brain urging her to refuse. He *seemed* safe enough, but ...

'I'm sorry,' she began uncomfortably, wishing she had not allowed him to open the car door, and then trying to soften her refusal by adding, 'I'm sure that your...your girlfriend will soon be back.'

Only she spoiled her attempt at assured sophistication by stammering a little over the words, and, far from having a palliative effect on him, to her trepidation they brought the anger back to his mouth as it tightened into a hard line.

He stared down at her, and demanded brusquely, 'My *what*?' His mouth tightened even more and he told her acidly, 'Trixie isn't my girlfriend. She's my niece. This isn't some idiotic lovers' tryst gone wrong, if that's what you're thinking, but a piece of deliberate manipulation.'

His mouth twisted suddenly and the look in his eyes was one of disgust.

'I realise that the circumstances here don't exactly encourage you to believe that I'm a perfectly respectable member of our local community, but do I *look* like the sort of idiot who'd go swimming with his girlfriend on a freezing cold autumn evening, and then let her walk off with his clothes? That kind of thing's for teenagers, not adults...'

To Harriet's surprise, he seemed more infuriated by her surely perfectly natural mistake about the nature of his predicament than by her refusal to give him a lift. Now that she looked at him a little more closely she saw that his face was that of a man who was more than likely rather autocratic, and used to controlling situations rather than to being controlled by them. Unlike her...but this was one occasion on which she intended to stand firm.

No matter how plausible and respectable he might seem, she would be a fool to give him a lift... She gave a tiny shiver, contemplating the kind of fate that could be hers, if he were not everything that he seemed.

Luckily she had kept the car engine running and now, as she looked nervously over her shoulder, wishing another car would appear on the quiet road, he seemed to read her mind.

'For God's sake, woman,' he said irately, 'do I *look* like a rapist?'

The look he gave her seemed to imply that, even if he were, he would scarcely choose the likes of her for a victim. Always sensitive to what she considered to be her own lack of sex appeal, a lack which she had always felt was underlined by

Louise's casual ability to attract men to her side like so many flies to honey, she flushed brilliantly and snapped at him, 'How do I know? I've never met one.' And then the acid look he gave her made her add uncomfortably, 'I'm sorry, but I *can't* give you a lift. You must see that. I could give someone a message, though...the local police?'

The look he gave her was as corrosive as acid.

A cool wind had sprung up, and even within the comfort of her small car she could feel its chill. No wonder that he, standing outside it, should suddenly shiver, his skin lifting in a rash of goose-bumps.

She almost weakened then, the caring, vulnerable nature which had been her undoing so often with Louise urging her to help him, but even as the words were forming on her tongue he was straightening up, his eyes brilliant with anger.

He said curtly, 'No, that won't be necessary,' and then, sketching her a swift and insulting half-bow that oddly enough did not make him look in the least ridiculous, he said sarcastically, 'That's what I like so much about the female sex—its compassion and understanding...'

And then, as she reached for the car door to close it, he lifted his hand and stopped her, the unexpected contact of his cool, damp fingers touching hers, almost like an electrical impulse passing through her body, freezing her into immobility as she stared at him, her heart pounding like that of a terrified rabbit.

'Do you really think that if I were intending you some harm I couldn't quite easily have overpowered you already? You know damn well I *don't* intend you any harm,' he added with soft bitterness, 'but, like the rest of your sex, you obviously enjoy torment for torment's sake. A small act of human charity, that's all I asked for.'

Her guilt increasing with every word he spoke, Harriet was just about to say she had changed her mind when, without warning, he removed his hand from hers and slammed the car door shut, leaving her feeling oddly bereft and hurt.

He had already turned his back on her and was disappearing in the direction from which he had come. Her car's headlights briefly picked out the lithe, powerfully male body, and then he was gone!

A shudder wrenched through her, and she realised that she was sitting there like someone in a trance.

Jerkily she put the car in gear and drove away.

Half an hour later, when her heartbeat had still not returned entirely to normal, she drove through the village, and slowed down carefully, looking for the lane which led to her cottage.

In the village she hesitated, wondering if she ought perhaps to report the incident to the police, anyway. Then, recognising that to do so would probably cause the man more embarrassment than relief, she did not stop.

Embarrassment... *she* had been the one to feel that, not him, she admitted wryly, remembering the shock of her first realisation that he was virtually nude. Strange how one accepted the sight of men on the beach wearing the briefest of attire without giving it a second thought, and yet when one was confronted by the same image in totally different surroundings——

She swallowed nervously, remembering how difficult she had found it to keep her eyes focused on the man's face without betraying her idiotic discomfort with his unclothed state. He should have been the one to feel discomposed, not her!

And as for telling her that it was his niece who was responsible for his plight... She frowned as she turned into the lane, forced to admit that both his anger and his words had held an undeniable ring of truth.

She had gained the impression that he was a man who did not have a particularly high opinion of the female sex. Why? she wondered. Given his looks, she would have thought that almost all his adult life he would have been surrounded by admiring women.

At last her car headlights picked out the shape of the cottage. It was properly dark now, and she wished yet again that she had not left it so late to leave London. There was something depressing about arriving alone and unwelcomed at her new home to find it all in darkness.

Apparently the cottage had originally been part of a large local estate, but had been sold off as being of no further use when the estate had been split up and sold several years ago, which accounted for the isolated position of the little house.

Previously it had been inhabited by the estate's gamekeeper, the agent had told her, and then, after the gamekeeper's death and until the estate had been broken up eighteen months earlier, the cottage had remained uninhabited.

Two local farmers had apparently bought most of the land, with the main house and its grounds being sold to a local businessman.

As Harriet unlocked the cottage door and switched on the lights, she felt a sense of relief. The light that flooded the small hall helped to banish the sense of apprehension and guilt that had filled her as she drove away from that uncomfortable interlude by the roadside.

Guilt ... Why should she feel guilt? She *had* offered to report his plight ...

She stood still, remembering the bitter look he had given her, his curt denunciation of her sex, and found herself hoping that, whoever he was, he lived far away enough to ensure that she didn't run into him again.

It was still relatively early, barely ten o'clock, and despite her long drive she was filled with a restless urgency that drove her not only to unpack her personal possessions from her car, but also to set up her typewriter on the table in the cottage's comfortably-sized kitchen-cum-living-room. There she started drafting out the beginnings of an idea which had occurred to her as she'd brought her things in.

Her furniture had arrived earlier in the week, and the relocation agency she had hired had ensured that it was installed exactly where she had wanted it. These last few days in a London hotel had not been particularly comfortable ones, but she had had an interview with her publisher yesterday morning and it had seemed pointless to move to her new home and then have to travel all the way back to London for a two-hour meeting.

She was soon deep in the grip of her work, and it was two hours before she stopped typing and realised how much her back and wrists were aching and how chilled she had become. Stifling a yawn, she put her typed papers tidily to one side and got up.

Time for bed now. She would check what she had written in the morning.

Smothering a second, wider yawn, she ensured that the doors were bolted and then made her way upstairs to the comfortable room with its sloping eaves, and its wonderful views of the rolling Border hills.

Her modern bed was out of place in these traditional surroundings. As soon as she could spare the time, she would have to comb the local antique shops for something more suitable, she decided tiredly as she prepared for bed.

This room with its sloping floor and uneven walls called for something heavy and old-fashioned—the sort of bed you virtually had to climb on to, the sort of bed that was stuffed with soft pillows, covered in crisp, lavender-scented cotton and topped with an old-fashioned faded quilt.

Everything was so quiet. Unlike London where the traffic never seemed to stop. Louise had told her scornfully that the silence would drive her mad and that she'd be back in London within six months, but she knew she wouldn't. Already she found something indescribably soothing and peaceful about the vague, muted noises the house made as it settled down around her... already she was looking forward to her new life.

She frowned, fighting off sleep. She just wished she hadn't met that man. His anger, his almost personal contempt of her, had struck a sour note she couldn't hush. She felt stupidly as though *she* were in some way responsible for causing that contempt, as though he had looked at her, had found her lacking as a woman, and for that reason had shown his contempt of her. Which was all quite ridiculous when he had made it quite plain that he disliked women in general.

She was still trying to puzzle out why she should go on thinking about him when she fell asleep.

She woke up abruptly, confused by unfamiliar sounds and by the vividness of her dreams, her face slightly pink as she tussled with the extraordinariness of her sleeping thoughts.

She had been walking alongside a river, engrossed in watching its flow, her ears and eyes attuned to its sounds and sights, and then suddenly without warning as she turned a corner she saw a man coming towards her. He was dressed casually in jeans and a cotton shirt, and as he came towards her and she saw the way he was looking at her, she realised in horrified shock that she was completely naked.

Every instinct clamoured to her to conceal herself from him, but it was already too late, and above the now urgent sound of the river she heard him saying mockingly, 'Now it's your turn... See how you like it...'

She shivered as she sat up in bed, trying to dismiss the symbolism of the dream. Outside it was raining, and heavily, raindrops spattering against her windows; the cause of the 'river' she had heard in her dream, perhaps?

Angry with herself for allowing an incident which she ought by now to have dismissed completely from her mind to occupy so much of her attention, she swung her legs out of bed, and decided that it was time she got up.

The relocation company had provided a certain amount of food, but there were things she would need, a certain amount of stocking up to do, which meant driving to the nearest market town.

Breakfast first and then she would make plans later, she decided, finding and filling the coffee filter and switching on the machine.

Two mugs of fragrant coffee and a piece of toast later, she decided that she might as well brave the wet weather and investigate a little of her immediate surroundings. From the field at the bottom of her wilderness of a garden, ran a footpath that went from the village right through up into the hills. Harriet didn't want to walk quite that far, but she decided that a breath of fresh air would help to settle her breakfast and her thoughts.

Pulling on her red boots, and adding a bright yellow shiny oilcloth jacket with a hood, she stepped outside.

Underfoot the ground was squelchy and muddy, and she was glad she had had the forethought to buy the boots. Her garden gate swung creakily as she opened it.

She walked through, across the lane and on to the footpath in the field beyond it.

CHAPTER TWO

HARRIET walked for almost half an hour without seeing or hearing anyone, in sheer bliss after London's frenetic streets and busy, uncaring crowds. She had learned a long time ago that it was possible to be far more lonely in the midst of a great press of humanity than it was in solitude, but she knew that Louise could never have understood her feelings.

She wished her sister well in her new life, and felt that this time she had found in her American husband a man who would give her order and direction.

Wrapped up in her bright yellow oilskin and her waterproof boots, Harriet was not bothered by the heavy rain and cool wind, and, walking past her overgrown garden, she smiled a little ruefully, remembering how in London she had dreamily planned to spend those hours when she wasn't writing in turning her small private wilderness into the kind of secret, romantic garden she had always dreamed of having.

Here, deep in this wet glade, it was impossible to look up clearly at the sky, but she suspected that the rain had set in for the day, which meant that, instead of wilfully wasting time walking, she ought to be at her typewriter. For the first of the four commissioned books her publishers had given her a deadline which should not prove too arduous to meet, but that did not mean that she could necessarily spend her time walking around dreamily in the rain, she told herself severely, deciding regretfully that it was time she returned to the cottage. She would have a certain amount of decorating to do over the next twelve months if she was to turn the cottage into the home she had envisaged, but decorating was a task she had set aside for the winter months.

Gardening...decorating...solitude...she was fast turning into the archetypal 'old maid' Louise had so often accused her of being. She would be thirty-five years old in three months' time. Not old precisely, but not young either, and age was after all a state of mind, and while a man of thirty-five and even of forty might be considered to be in his prime, for a woman—even in these liberated days... She stopped walking, and found that somehow or other, without her knowing how it had happened, a mental image of a tall, dark, and very damp man had slipped into her head and refused to leave it. A very male man...a very angry man...a man who had plainly not seen her as a desirable woman at all, but rather as an object of irritation and contempt.

Would it really have hurt her to give him a lift? A neighbourly act of charity and kindness? Had the years of living in London, celibate, alone in so many ways, and with so many responsibilities, turned her into the kind of timid, over-imaginative single woman who thought that every man she met represented some kind of danger?

She didn't like the picture her thoughts were drawing, and dismissed it as irrational. Of course she had been quite right to refuse his request. The police via the media were constantly warning women about the dangers inherent in exactly the kind of situation she had found herself in last night. No, she had nothing to reproach herself with, and yet—— Her reverie was abruptly shattered as a large and very muddy chocolate-brown Labrador suddenly came crashing through the undergrowth towards her, hotly pursued by a small, slim red-haired girl, bare-headed despite the rain, and dressed in enviably well-worn and well-used dark green jacket, faded jeans and dark green wellingtons.

'Come here at once, Ben,' she shouted to the dog, her eyes rounding in surprise as she saw Harriet.

'Oh! I didn't know anyone else was here—I thought that Ben had got the scent of a rabbit. He never catches them, thank goodness, but I'm in enough trouble already, without having to spend half the morning chasing him all over the country-side. Oh, no, Ben...down, you bad dog!'

It was too late. Ben, evidently a gregarious animal, had flung himself enthusiastically at Harriet, almost knocking her over in the process, and was now proceeding to lick her, despite the girl's attempts to call him to heel.

Harriet didn't mind. She loved dogs and always had done. In London it had been impossible to keep one, but perhaps here...

'Oh, dear, I *am* sorry,' the girl apologised, rushing up to Harriet to rescue her from her pet.

She had wide-set hazel eyes, a *retroussé* nose, and the kind of warm smile that illuminated her whole face. She looked about sixteen or seventeen, and

Harriet guessed probably had the kind of quick, almost intuitive intelligence that matched her manner. Altogether something of an enchantress, who would probably drive the male sex mad once she was old enough to recognise her own power, Harriet reflected, gently pushing the dog down and holding on to his collar for her.

'Oh, goodness, look what he's done to your jacket!' The girl grimaced guiltily.

The front of Harriet's yellow oilskin was covered in muddy pawprints, but she shook her head in dismissal of another apology.

'They'll wash off, there's no real harm done.'

'Thank goodness for that,' her companion said with disarming frankness. 'All I need right now is someone to go complaining to Rigg about me. I'm in enough trouble as it is.' She rolled her eyes theatrically, and giggled. 'Right at this moment, I'm supposed to be in my room contemplating my sins. Have you ever heard anything so archaic? Rigg really is the end. I keep on telling him I'm an adult, not a child.'

Her mouth became stubborn and resolute all of a sudden, striking a vague chord of memory within Harriet. She frowned a little herself, but before she could say anything the girl was speaking again.

'I'm Trixie Matthews, by the way, and this, as you've probably guessed, is Ben.'

Trixie. An unusual name, and now she had heard it twice within one single span of twenty-four hours... Not merely coincidence, surely? Could *this* be the niece of whom the man who had stopped her car last night had spoken so furiously?

The tempation to find out was almost over-whelming; it wouldn't have been difficult, not with this girl, with her confiding, open nature, but Harriet had a very strict personal moral code, and to ask the questions teeming through her brain would undoubtedly break it—and, besides, what did it matter? Last night's interlude by the roadside was over and done with, and had already occupied far too many of her thoughts.

Giving the girl a polite, dismissive smile, she turned round ready to head back to the cottage. The smile was one she had perfected over the years, for keeping other people at a distance, but the girl seemed unaware of that fact, and fell into step beside her. Ben, the Labrador, having drawn his mistress's attention to the stranger in their midst, was apparently quite content to snuffle in the undergrowth a few yards ahead of them.

'Are you staying in the village?' Trixie asked Harriet interestedly. 'Not that we've had much of a summer this year.' She pulled a face. 'I keep telling Rigg that I need a proper holiday.' She gave Harriet a mischievous smile.

'He's so stuffy and old-fashioned... Loads of girls my age are *living* on their own, never mind going on holiday with a friend and her mother.'

Many girls were, Harriet acknowledged, but not girls like this one, whose every word and gesture betrayed how cherished and protected she was.

'Where are you staying? At the Staple?'

The Staple was the village's ancient pub, with a history dating back to the times when the village had been one of the staging posts on the long trek south to English markets for the shepherds who raised their flocks on the Border hills. Hence its name.

'No...actually, I'm not a visitor. I've just moved up here from London.'

'You've *moved* up here?' Trixie's expression said quite obviously that she was surprised. 'From London, but... You must have bought the old gamekeeper's cottage, then. Rigg said it had been sold. To a schoolteacher.'

The girl was frowning now, and for some reason she couldn't truly explain, Harriet found herself saying, 'I used to teach. I don't now.'

She didn't say what she did instead, and Trixie's frown disappeared, to be replaced with a wide grin.

'Thank goodness for that, otherwise Rigg would probably try to persuade you to give me extra lessons during the holidays.' She pulled a face again. 'He's got this obsession about keeping me occupied. Just because both my parents were up at Oxford.' She pulled another face. 'I keep on telling Rigg that *they* may have been brilliant, but I'm not. Don't *you* think that, at almost eighteen, I'm old enough to go on holiday with a girlfriend and her mother, without Rigg kicking up such a fuss?' she then demanded indignantly.

Harriet, who suspected there was something she wasn't being told, could only offer a gentle palliative. 'Perhaps, but if your uncle has refused to give his permission...'

'Refused! I thought he was going to have forty fits,' Trixie told her gloomily, 'and all because of a silly mistake. I tried to tell him what had happened, but he wouldn't listen, and then I tried to *show* him how easily circumstances can be misinterpreted, but instead of understanding what I was trying to prove he was furious with me...'

Indignation showed in the hazel eyes, and Harriet felt a sudden surge of sympathy for her uncle. The responsibility of a girl like this one could not be an easy one.

Trixie gave another faint sigh. 'I suppose I'd better get back before he discovers I've broken out. Of course, he wouldn't be like this at all if he wasn't such a mis...such a missy...one of those men who hate women,' she elucidated, leaving Harriet to supply the word automatically.

'You mean a misogynist.'

'Mmm...and all because some woman walked out on him years ago,' Trixie told her, with all the scorn of youth.

Harriet knew she shouldn't be listening to any of this, never mind wanting, almost encouraging the next confidence.

'Of course, I suppose it wasn't very nice, virtually being left at the altar, so to speak,' Trixie allowed.

Left at the altar! Harriet blinked, wondering if after all she had jumped to erroneous conclusions about the identity of Trixie's uncle. She couldn't imagine any woman leaving at the altar the man she had met last night.

They were back in sight of her cottage and, guiltily aware that by rights she should have stopped Trixie's confidences some time ago, she gave the girl another smile, and said quietly, 'It's been nice meeting you... I hope your uncle isn't too angry when he finds out you've been out.'

'Oh, Rigg doesn't get *angry*. He just sort of looks at you...you know, as though you're the lowest of the low. I suppose it's true that I'm a bit of a trial to him. That's what Mrs Arkwright, our housekeeper, says. She thinks the world of Rigg, and not a lot of me. I heard her telling her husband—he's the gardener—that Rigg was a saint for taking me on after my parents were killed... A saint! He's more like a devil,' Trixie told her acidly. 'He just can't seem to understand that I'm almost eighteen...grown up... I like your outfit by the way,' she added inconsequentially. 'Rigg would have a fit if I bought anything like that.'

She scowled rebelliously at her own serviceable and eminently suitable country clothes, and it occurred to Harriet that had she herself been dressed in her normal sober clothes, this girl would probably never have been quite so forthcoming with her.

A twinge of guilt attacked her. She ought not to have allowed Trixie to tell her so much. Rigg! It was an unusual name. She longed to ask how he had come by it, but, although she suspected Trixie would have been quite willing to tell her, she firmly resisted the temptation.

They parted at Harriet's garden gate, but later in the day, as she laboured over the outline for her new book, Harriet found it increasingly hard to subdue a sub-plot which involved a slender red-headed girl with hazel eyes, a confiding manner, and an ogre of an uncle.

In the end she gave way to it, and before the day was over she discovered that her book had changed direction completely, and that her plot had been taken over by her new characters.

It was four o'clock before she remembered that she had intended to go shopping.

The market town was a good three-quarters of an hour's drive away. She had enough food for tonight ... She looked at the telephone, trying to work out the time difference between England and California, wondering if she should ring Louise and check that she had settled into her new life happily, and then she dismissed the instinct, telling herself that Louise was an adult with a husband to take care of her. Odd, how, whenever she thought of Louise, she always thought of her in terms of needing to be looked after, when in truth Louise was far more resilient than she was—far more adaptable, far more able to take care of herself. Emotionally, at least.

As Harriet pushed away her typewriter, an unfamiliar sense of happiness filled her. Freedom ... freedom to be what she wanted ... to do what she wanted ... with no other claims on her time or her emotions, with no need to put others first. It was the kind of hedonistic bliss that was totally unfamiliar to her, and, on the strength of it, she donned her wellingtons and her oilskin for the second time that day and marched purposefully out into the wilderness, where she spent a profitable and very muddy hour removing weeds from the crazy paving path that ran along the length of the front garden to the gate, before the growing dusk drove her inside.

Her work in the garden had produced hunger pangs which sent her straight to have a bath and prepare a meal.

The heavy rainclouds had brought an earlier dusk than might have been expected, and, having listened to the news and a weather forecast that suggested that the rain was going to continue for a few days, Harriet retired to bed with a shiny-covered, deliciously smelling, luxurious hardback copy of the latest book by one of her favourite authors.

However, for once the author's skill failed to occupy all her attention and she found her mind wandering recklessly back not just to her meeting earlier in the day with Trixie Matthews but also to that unexpected exchange with her uncle.

'Trixie,' he had called her before realising his mistake, with anger and resignation in his voice. Poor man, it couldn't be easy for him, apparently totally responsible for such a spirited teenager.

She fell asleep on the thought, a soft smile curling her mouth as she wondered how on earth even so obviously enterprising and resourceful a girl as Trixie had got a man like Rigg to strip down to his underwear in the first place, never mind leaving him stranded without either any clothes or any transport!

Well, supermarkets were obviously something that remained the same countrywide, Harriet reflected tiredly, as she collected her receipt from the girl on the checkout and wheeled her trolley out into the murky greyness of the wet autumn day and the unprepossessing expanse of the supermarket's car park.

Had the day been pleasanter, she might have been tempted to explore a little more of the town, but the rain was falling heavily, and she felt chilled by the icy wind that whipped across the exposed tarmac.

So much for the mellow fruitfulness of autumn, she thought wryly as she packed her shopping away in the car and then drove away.

The Border hills looked bleak and alien as she drove homewards, and inside the warm capsule of her car Harriet shivered. She didn't envy anyone working on those hills today, where the sheep would be protected from the rain by their oily coats, but the shepherds and their dogs...

The village was deserted, and she remembered that the agent had told her that Tuesday was their early closing day. Early closing...she smiled to herself. Living in London, she had almost forgotten that such things existed. She stopped the car to allow an old man to cross the road, watching him disappear into the old-fashioned telephone kiosk.

The wind buffeted her when she stopped the car on her drive and hurried to unlock the back door. Once it was unlocked she removed the keys and threw them and her handbag on to the kitchen table so that she could hurry back to get her shopping in.

The slam of the back door as she ran back to the car meant nothing to her until she returned to it, her arms fully occupied with the heavy cardboard box of groceries, and discovered that it wouldn't yield one single inch to the pressure of her arm on the handle.

Telling herself not to panic, she put down the box and tried the handle again, realising too late, when the door wouldn't open, that she had forgotten to snick back the Yale lock after opening the door, and that her keys were now locked inside the house and she and her groceries were locked outside it.

As she stood staring in self-condemnatory disbelief at the locked door, she suddenly realised that she was getting soaking wet. Staring at the door and expecting it to open by sheer will-power wasn't going to work and, London-trained, she had of course made sure that all her windows were closed and locked before she went out.

So now what was she to do?

The agent? He might have a spare key. Failing that, he would be able to recommend a locksmith, perhaps...

Groaning to herself, she picked up the now damp cardboard box and shoved it back in the car, thankful that she had not yet had time to add her car keys to the same ring as her house keys.

The nearest telephone was in the village, and the thought that without them she would have had to walk the two miles there in this weather, dressed in her flimsy jacket and her court shoes, made her shiver even more than she was already doing.

The village and the telephone box were both empty. She had to ask for directory enquiries in order to get the agent's number. Fortunately she could remember his address as well as his name.

His secretary listened to her problem and then told her sympathetically that he was out and not due back for over an hour. 'Wait a minute, though,' she added as Harriet was about to hang up. 'I seem to remember that they held a spare key up at the Hall, because they were keeping an eye on the place while it was empty. Do you want me to ring through to them and check?'

Harriet thanked her and said no, explaining that she had her car and it would probably be quicker for her to drive straight round to the Hall and find out for herself.

She knew where it was, for the agent had pointed out to her the impressive wrought-iron gateway, fronting on to the main road a couple of miles past her own unkempt lane. As she thanked the girl for her help and hurried back to her car, Harriet could only pray that the Hall's spare key had not yet been returned to the agent, and was glad that she herself had not had time to change the locks as she had fully intended to do.

Cursing herself for her own stupidity, she drove back through the village, past the entrance to her own lane, and on towards the immaculate, black-painted wrought-iron gates with their gold tips, and impressive crest.

The man who had bought the Hall, in what the agent had described to her as a very rundown state indeed, had apparently been almost as much a stranger to the area as she was herself, a very successful businessman whose ancestors had originally come from this part of the world, the agent had told her. He had gone on to explain that not only had this man bought the Hall and moved into it, but also he had transferred his business to the area as well, opening up a new factory on the small industrial estate just outside the market town.

'Something or other in computers he is,' Harriet had been told, and was glad that she had kept to herself her own method of earning her living. The agent did not mean any harm, but he obviously couldn't resist discussing his clients, and she was still too unsure of her own ability to follow up her first novel with an acceptable second one to feel she justified being described as 'a writer'.

She had to get out of her car to open the gates, but was too relieved to discover that they were not electronically controlled and thus impenetrable to her to care about the discomfort of getting even wetter.

Her thin jacket, adequate enough while she only had to dash from the car to the supermarket, was now soaked through, the dampness penetrating the thin T-shirt she was wearing underneath it, making her skin feel cold and clammy.

Her jeans were wet as well, the heavy denim fabric rubbing uncomfortably against her skin every time she had to change gear.

The Hall was not the imposing edifice she had anticipated, but a long, low, rambling affair of a similar period to her own cottage. Even with its stone walls soaked dark grey by the heavy rain to match the surrounding countryside, it still managed to exude an air of welcome and tranquillity.

Its warmth and beauty, indefinable and yet so very much there, took her breath away for a moment, so that she forgot the discomfort of her damp clothes and even momentarily forgot the irritation of locking herself out of the cottage, and the embarrassment of announcing as much to the strangers who lived here.

As she stepped out of the car and walked towards the ancient oak door, she found herself envying whoever it was who lived here—not because of the house's size and privacy, but for its marvellous and totally unexpected aura of peace and happiness.

Someone was opening the door as she approached it. Trixie's familiar, smiling face greeted her, the younger girl apparently completely unsurprised to see her.

Ben, the Labrador, welcomed her boisterously as Trixie almost pulled her inside.

'I'm so glad you've come round,' Trixie told her. 'I've been bored out of my mind.' She rolled her eyes and giggled. 'Rigg has virtually banned me from going out.'

They were standing in a lovely square panelled hallway, with an enormous stone fireplace that actually had a fire burning in its grate.

Ben, having welcomed her, went and lay down in front of it with a luxurious sigh of pleasure.

A worn oak staircase went up one wall to a galleried landing, the staircase wall lined with paintings which looked frighteningly as though they might be originals and priceless.

Heavy damask curtains hung at the windows, their rich fabric adding an extra glow of warmth to the room. She was standing, Harriet belatedly recognised, on an antique rug that was surely never intended to be the recipient of wet and probably still muddy shoes.

She started to apologise automatically, but Trixie just laughed.

'Come on. I'm dying to introduce you to Rigg. He's always complaining that I never make any respectable friends...'

Harriet froze as the potential embarrassment of the situation struck her. Somehow or other she had assumed that Trixie's uncle would not be here, that he would be at work. If he *was* the same man she had had that difficult confrontation with the other evening, she had no wish at all to meet him again, especially not under these circumstances—not an invited and welcome guest to his home, but rather a petitioner.

'Oh, no...please...there's no need to disturb your uncle. I'm sure he must be very busy,' she protested, catching hold of Trixie's arm and adding uncomfortably, 'Actually I didn't come here to see you, Trixie. I didn't even realise you lived here.' Although she ought to have done, she recognised; it had been obvious from Trixie's engaging and informative conversation that she came from a wealthy background, and from what the agent had told her about the owner of the Hall she ought perhaps to have had the sense to put two and two together and recognise that it must be Trixie's home. No wonder her uncle hadn't wanted Harriet reporting his plight to the police.

Trixie looked at her, her expression clouding a little.

'You haven't come to see me, then?'

Quickly Harriet explained about locking herself out of her cottage.

'I rang the agent I bought the house from, and his secretary told me that you used to have a key here.'

Neither of them heard someone also enter the room, but as Trixie furrowed her forehead and then said doubtfully, 'I don't know anything about it. I'll have to ask Rigg.'

Then an all-too-familiar male voice sent shivers of despair racing down Harriet's spine as it enquired dulcetly, 'You'll have to ask me what, Trixie?'

Without intending to, Harriet swung round towards the door, and suffered a heart-shaking jolt of sensation as she stared at the man standing there. He seemed familiar and yet almost totally unfamiliar in his formal business suit and immaculate white shirt.

The dark hair, no longer damp and clinging to his scalp but well cut and brushed, seemed to accentuate the maleness of a face which in the daylight she could see appeared to be almost carved in deep lines of cynicism.

'It's Harriet,' Trixie told him. 'She's locked herself out of the cottage and she thought we might have a spare key.'

For a moment, from the dismissive way his glance flicked over her and then returned with hard intent to his niece, Harriet thought that he had not after all recognised her.

She was surprised by the strength of her chagrin that he, who had made such a dangerously lasting impression on her, had apparently no remembrance of her whatsoever.

'Try for a slightly more logical explanation, Trixie,' he suggested calmly. Although Trixie grimaced a little, it was obvious to Harriet that she had a healthy respect for her uncle, because after gritting her teeth and casting Harriet an appealing glance, she said quickly, 'This is Harriet, Rigg. I met her the other...yesterday. She lives in the old game-keeper's cottage. Harriet, this is my uncle.'

'Thank you, Trixie, Miss Smith and I have already met.'

Harriet started a little. Then she had been wrong in that first assumption that he had not recognised her, but how had he discovered her surname?

'Oh, have you?' Trixie gave them both a puzzled look, and said to Harriet, 'You never said anything yesterday about meeting Rigg.'

It was Rigg who answered for her, saying silkily, 'Perhaps the incident is not one she cares to recall. Miss Smith was, I'm afraid, the unfortunate victim of your idiotic behaviour the other evening. She has the misfortune to drive a car of the same make and colour as yours. When I emerged from the river, to discover her driving towards me, I thought for a moment that you'd come to your senses.'

As she glanced at Trixie, Harriet saw that that unrepentant young lady was trying hard not to laugh. Her uncle obviously didn't share her amusement, though. He was looking grimly at both of them.

'Oh, Harriet, no! Was it you who refused to give Rigg a lift?' Trixie gasped, before her mirth overcame her. 'See, it worked after all, Rigg!' she crowed to her uncle. 'Circumstantial evidence...and I'll bet that Harriet didn't believe——'

'What Miss Smith believed was that I was either a lunatic or a rapist, or possibly both,' Rigg interrupted Trixie in a hard voice.

'Oh, Harriet, how brave of you—refusing to give him a lift.' Trixie's eyes danced with laughter.

But Harriet couldn't share her innocent amusement. Then Rigg had been the one to ask a favour of her, and she had refused, had refused to help or assist him, and now their positions were reversed, and she was the one needing his help... She shuddered inwardly, and wished it had been anyone else in the world she was having to confront right now rather than this cold, stern man. And even more than that she wished that her hitherto easily controllable imagination would not choose now of all times to become both rebellious and dangerous, by insisting on substituting for his immaculate business suit and shirt the vivid memory of how she had seen him in the headlights of her car, wearing nothing but...

She swallowed hard, and said huskily, 'I'm sorry to have disturbed you, but the agent *did* say that you might have a spare key for the cottage here at one time, and I was wondering if you still had it?'

CHAPTER THREE

HARRIET knew the answer before the man gave it, of course. It had been there for her to see, quite clearly, in the quick gleam of satisfaction that lightened the coldness of his eyes to a momentary burning gold. It came as no real surprise to her to hear him saying coolly, 'Unfortunately it was returned to the agent by my secretary some days ago. It's probably still in the post.'

She had no doubt that he was telling the truth: this was not a man who would ever stoop to deceit, for any purpose, even one such as retribution. Harriet frowned without knowing she was doing so, her concentration not on the man watching her but on the sharp insistence of her own thoughts. How had she come by such an intense awareness of this man? Why did she have this gut-deep sensation of knowing what kind of human being he was? It wasn't a knowledge she welcomed. It was too dangerous, too overpowering...too threatening.

Realising that both he and Trixie were looking at her, she gave them both a brief, polite smile, the kind of smile she had used all her adult life to hold strangers at bay, an aloof, distancing smile that brought a touch of bewilderment to Trixie's eyes.

'Oh, but surely, Rigg, you could do *something*?' Trixie insisted, glancing from one set face to the other, half sensing the friction between them.

'No, really,' Harriet protested quickly. 'I didn't really think there was much chance that you would still have a key, but it was worth a try.'

She turned to leave, conscious of her damp, unkempt appearance and its direct contrast to that of the man watching her, conscious too of an intense feminine awareness and reaction to him as a man that for a moment brought her to a dead stop, her body going rigid with rejection of what she was feeling.

Sexual awareness of Rigg Matthews? Ridiculous. She thought back along her life and those occasions when she had ached to feel just that kind of response for the nice, kind men she had occasionally dated...that she had so often wished she might feel for Paul and never had.

She had decided years ago that she was not the kind of woman who was ever going to feel or experience that kind of intense sexual responsiveness, and yet out of the blue, in the most unexpected and unwanted circumstances, here it was, sharp and painful, powerful enough to hold her body still while her bewildered brain focused on the stealth and speed of the sensation which had overtaken her.

A tiny shiver broke over her, and she was free of the momentary paralysis, feeling oddly weak, lightheaded almost. She was deeply thankful that she had her back to Rigg.

The potential humiliation of having him recognise that brief flaring of feminine arousal was enough to make her walk quickly towards the door, anxious to escape from his presence just as soon as she could.

She hadn't even realised that Trixie had followed her, until the younger girl reached out breathlessly to stop her opening the door, and said urgently, 'No, wait... I'm sure there's something Rigg can do, to help.'

She looked appealingly at her uncle as she spoke, and Harriet saw that, despite her criticism and the rebellion she had expressed to Harriet the other morning, she loved and respected him and, further, she obviously felt able to totally rely on him, to call upon his help. In her face was the sure and certain knowledge that, no matter what problems life caused her, Rigg could solve them, and thinking of her own life Harriet envied her a little.

Louise had always been their parents' favourite, and from quite young Harriet had learned that she must fight her own battles in life.

Still, self-reliance was no bad thing, she told herself sturdily, the polite, conventional words of denial coming placidly to her lips as she said coolly, 'That's very kind of you, Trixie, but I'm sure your uncle would be the first to agree that there's really very little he can do that I can't do myself.'

She had unconsciously adopted the crisp, firm voice she had used at school. Her manner was polite but distant as she added lightly, 'It's really just a matter of finding a locksmith. I intend to drive into Hawick, and——'

It was a pity that a sudden and uncontrollable fit of shivers shook her violently, followed by an unstoppable sneeze. A cold! That was the last thing she needed right now.

Her voice suspended, she fumbled in her pocket for a handkerchief and then heard Rigg saying coolly, 'If I could offer a suggestion...I seem to recall that the cottage has a small window let into the loft.'

'Yes,' Harriet agreed. Shock made her turn round and look at him, and then wish that she hadn't. For all his austerity and remoteness, he really was the most extraordinarily good-looking man. She wondered at the folly of the girl who had apparently left him at the altar, and then chided herself. A warm heart and a generous mind were more important attributes than good looks, and on the evidence so far it did not seem that Rigg possessed either of them.

'Yes...yes, there is,' she answered automatically, 'but——'

'I was going to suggest that it might be an idea to break in through that window. It would possibly save time.' He looked her up and down, in a way that made her cringingly aware of the picture she must present, with her hair in rats' tails, her nose pink, her jeans soaking and clinging to her legs.

It might have been the awareness of how unpleasantly cold and damp she felt that made her shiver a second time, or it might not. She saw the way Rigg's mouth tightened—with distaste, no doubt—and then she remembered uncomfortably how she had left him standing out in the open clad in far less than she was wearing right now, and even more damp.

She forced herself to summon another polite smile.

'The loft. Yes, well, thank you. I'll try that.'

The look he gave her made her feel as though she were closer to Trixie's age than his own.

'Not without a ladder and someone to hold it for you, you won't,' he told her promptly. Then, without taking his eyes off her, he added, 'Trixie, go into the kitchen, will you, and ask Mrs Arkwright if she can rustle up a hot drink for our guest.' And then, as though he knew she was going to protest, he continued inexorably, 'And after you've done that perhaps you could take Harriet upstairs and find her something dry to wear. In the meantime, Tom and I will drive over to the cottage and see if we can get in.'

Talk about having coals of fire heaped on her head, Harriet fumed. At one masterly stroke she had been both reduced to a child of Trixie's age or less, and also made aware of her own lack of charity in refusing to help him.

Seething with anger and embarrassment, she wondered if he had deliberately allowed her to think he was going to retaliate by not helping her, just so that he could have the pleasure of what she strongly suspected was an overt act of *noblesse oblige*.

Whatever the reasons, she was damned if she was going to accept his act of charity. She opened her mouth to tell him as much, and promptly sneezed a second time.

By the time she had blown her nose, he was gone, and Trixie was on her way to the kitchen.

Half an hour later Harriet was ruefully surveying her reflection in the outsize sweatshirt Trixie had given her and the skin-tight jeans that went underneath it, her hair dry, but so softened by the rain that she couldn't do anything with it other than allow it to fall on to her shoulders in silky disarray.

Mrs Arkwright insisted on providing her with a bowl of her home-made soup, so deliciously filling and warming that Harriet wasn't able to resist it.

Rigg's housekeeper was a homely, friendly woman, who confessed to Harriet that Miss Trixie could be something of a handful, but that Rigg was the most considerate employer she had ever had.

Sensing that the older woman was curious about her, Harriet felt obliged to give her a little of her own history.

'London,' she said, shaking her head. 'I've never been able to understand why anyone should want to live in a place like that. Up here now... well, a body can breathe decently, if you know what I mean.'

Harriet did, and she found herself confiding to the older woman how thrilled she had been to be able to fulfil her dream of living in the country.

Trixie, who had left the kitchen to take a phone call from one of her friends, came back in just as Harriet was explaining how Louise's marriage had freed her to sell her London home and move north.

'Leave London? You must have been mad,' Trixie told her forthrightly, making Harriet smile and Mrs Arkwright shake her head.

'That was Eva on the phone,' she told them. 'Her mother wants to know if I'm going away with them in the Christmas holidays. I told her I'm still working on Rigg.'

'Now, Miss Trixie, you know full well he won't let you go,' Mrs Arkwright told her, adding to Harriet, 'Nor do I blame him either. A real wild set that Mrs Soames goes around with.'

Trixie made a disgusted sound in her throat.

'The trouble with Rigg is that he doesn't understand what modern life's all about,' she complained to Harriet. 'He's still living in the dark ages,' she finished in a disgusted voice.

Remembering the quarrels she herself had had with Louise, Harriet felt a momentary stirring of sympathy for Rigg. It wasn't something she wanted, this fellow-feeling for a man whom every sense of preservation she possessed warned her it would be dangerous to allow to occupy too many of her thoughts. Besides, it was obvious to her that Trixie had an essential sweetness of nature that was completely lacking in Louise.

'Don't worry,' Trixie told her comfortingly, mistaking the reason for her small frown. 'Rigg will find some way of getting in.'

She glanced out of the kitchen window and grimaced. 'Just look at that rain. We've hardly had any summer, and John Beard was saying last week that we're in for a hard winter. He used to be a shepherd, but he's retired now,' she explained to Harriet. 'I wish Rigg would let me go skiing with Eva and her mother. I *need* a holiday!'

Harriet laughed, but Mrs Arkwright told her severely, 'If you ask me, it's your uncle who needs the holiday.'

'Well, there's nothing to stop him coming with us. I asked him if he would, but you know what he's like. He said he was too busy!'

Mrs Arkwright snorted unsympathetically, and returned to Harriet, exclaiming, 'It's no wonder Rigg doesn't trust that Mrs Soames—letting that boyfriend of hers bring you home, and him driving his car when he'd been drinking, by all accounts!

I don't blame Rigg for being angry, especially when Mrs Soames had promised she'd have you back here by eleven o'clock. Gone two in the morning it was when you got back, and for myself I'd as soon trust that manfriend of hers as I would a rabid dog,' Mrs Arkwright finished forthrightly.

There was a highly charged pause. Trixie looked rebelliously at the housekeeper, and, almost without realising she was doing it, Harriet stepped into the uncomfortable silence.

'I expect there was a good reason why Mrs Soames didn't get Trixie back home in time——' she said calmly.

'Yes, there was,' Trixie interrupted her eagerly.

But Harriet continued, 'But it's also easy to understand why your uncle should have been concerned and angry.'

Trixie's face fell again. Telling herself that it was none of her business, Harriet tensed as she heard a car drive past.

'That will be Rigg,' Trixie announced, her anger with him apparently forgotten as she jumped up and ran to the door. 'I hope he's managed to break in.'

So did Harriet.

When the two men walked into the kitchen, her glance went automatically to Rigg. There was a small cut on his left hand, and a cobweb clinging to the arm of his jacket. Without realising she was doing it, she gnawed on her bottom lip, tension gripping her body as she stood up.

'Did you manage to get in, Rigg?' Trixie asked him, beating her to the question.

'Yes.' He turned to Harriet and said, almost sternly, 'You'll have to have a lock put on the attic window when you have it replaced. I'm not sure whether your insurance policy will cover its repair.'

He reached into his pocket and handed her her keys, his face grim.

'We've boarded up the attic window, and it should be weatherproof for a few days, but I'd advise you to get it repaired as soon as possible. The farmers' weather bulletin for the area was forecasting gales in the next week.'

Dumbly Harriet took the keys from him, feeling like a chastised child. It made her summon her forces of control and maturity and say firmly, 'Thank you for your help. It was stupid of me to lock myself out, but I'm not completely without common sense. Naturally I'll get the roof-light repaired as soon as possible.'

She saw that he was still frowning, although it took her a couple of seconds to realise that it wasn't her face he was looking at but her body, and instantly she became conscious of the picture she must present in Trixie's borrowed clothes, with her hair hanging down her back, more like a teenager than a sensible woman of almost thirty-five.

As she took the keys from him, her fingertips touched his briefly. They were warm and hard, and a disturbing sensation raced through her body, freezing her where she stood. Trixie was talking to her uncle, saying something about her phone call. He turned his head to look at her. Immediately Harriet pulled away from him, and headed for the door.

The sooner she was back in her own cottage and away from his disturbing presence, the better. She would have to return Trixie's borrowed clothes, of course, but she would telephone first, and try to make sure that Rigg wasn't going to be around.

A misogynist was how Trixie had described him. He was an intelligent man and surely couldn't be unaware of the effect he was likely to have on members of her sex. She didn't want him getting the idea that her visits to the house were deliberately contrived to bring herself to his attention.

Always sensitive where her own looks and apparent lack of sexuality were concerned, Harriet could all too well imagine what a man of his looks and wealth would think of a woman like her. Since she had turned thirty she had endured too many gibes from Louise about her single, sexless state to have any illusions about how other people saw her.

Programmed by her parents to think of herself as inferior in femininity to her sister, she had no awareness of the fact that it was her protectively cool distancing of herself from the world in general, and the male sex in particular, which had led to her celibate lifestyle and not, as she believed, a lack of something intrinsic and female within herself.

When her guard was down, she was far more attractive than she knew: delicately feminine, with a vulnerability that appealed to the basic male hunting instinct.

She saw that Rigg had switched his attention back from Trixie to herself, and that he was frowning at her again. No doubt anxious for her to be gone, she acknowledged, as she fumbled with the door handle.

But to her astonishment, he said curtly, 'I'll follow you home. It's getting dark, and although we locked up securely behind us these days you never know who might be lurking about. The boarding we put over that roof-light wouldn't keep out a determined intruder.'

Harriet stared at him.

'Oh, no, I'm sure I'll be all right. I've caused you enough trouble already.'

'It's no use,' Trixie warned her. 'Rigg has this overdeveloped belief that we women can't take care of ourselves.'

Her chin tilted aggressively as she spoke, but Rigg refused to rise to the bait, instead following Harriet to the door, so that she had no choice but to precede him through it.

As they walked to their respective cars—his, she noticed, a heavyweight and eminently practical Range Rover—she ached to be able to apologise to him for not helping him out the night they had met, but was unable to form the words that would sound right.

She was all too uncomfortably aware of how flustered and on edge she felt in his presence, petrified that he might somehow divine the cause of the riot of unfamiliar sensations his presence aroused within her. She couldn't understand what was happening to her. It was so unlike her to react like this, and he had certainly given her no encouragement to do so. Quite the opposite.

Normally a competent driver, she fumbled over starting the car and then ground the gears so horribly that her face burned at the idea of what Rigg must be thinking of her, but at last she had her small car in motion and was driving back to her cottage.

The darkness of the rainclouds had brought on an early false dusk, and the cottage, set in its shrouding of trees, looked dark and lonely.

She gave a small shiver as she stopped the car. The first thing she intended to do tomorrow was to have some spare keys cut. As she got out of her car she saw Rigg emerging from his. Her knees shook a little as she forced herself to thank him formally for his help. She couldn't bring herself to look at him properly. He had had every good reason not to help her, and yet he had done so.

He had brought a torch out of his Range Rover with him and now he shone it upwards, almost immediately finding the roof-light.

'Nothing seems to have been disturbed,' he announced. 'But if you'd like me to come in and check...'

'No, no, that won't be necessary,' Harriet told him hastily, stepping back from him so quickly that she slipped off the edge of the path and started to overbalance.

Rigg reacted immediately, dropping the torch and reaching out to steady her, his hands closing firmly on her upper arms as he jerked her back to her feet, almost lifting her bodily back on to the path.

Beneath the shock of the unexpected physical contact she felt a startled flash of awareness of his strength. He had lifted her as effortlessly as though she were still a child, but then, as she had good reason to know, the body beneath that expensive business suit was leanly fit and extremely well-muscled.

As though he felt the shock that rippled through her, the fingers fastened around her upper arms tightened momentarily. The headlights of the Range Rover showed his dark profile bent towards her, his mouth thinning with what she suspected was dislike.

'You're quite safe,' he told her curtly. 'Despite the impression that my niece has undoubtedly given you as to the dastardliness of my nature, I assure you that my failings do not run to inclinations to rape.'

It ought to have been the easiest thing in the world for her to have reassured him with at least some semblance of sophistication that she had no such fears, but instead, for some stupid reason, she started to tremble helplessly, causing his frown to deepen and his intent gaze to search her face.

'It was a joke,' he told her drily, and then added surprisingly, 'I'm sorry if I alarmed you.'

He released her carefully, and stepped back from her, making her feel even more of a fool.

'I'm almost thirty-five years old, not fifteen,' she told him huskily. 'And I'm not that much of a fool.' Even if she had given him the impression that she might be.

Her own mouth tightened a fraction, and for some reason he seemed to focus on it for the space of a handful of seconds. Her heartbeat seemed almost entirely suspended for the same length of time.

His eyebrows rose.

'I should have thought that these days no woman could easily feel that her age protected her from such an attack.'

He was almost reproving her, leaving her feeling exasperated enough to say uncautiously, 'That wasn't what I meant.'

'No? What did you mean then?'

How on earth had she got herself into this situation? She floundered for a moment, and then said grimly, 'What I meant was that you do not strike me as the kind of man who would need to resort to rape to... to...'

She was floundering again, but fortunately he didn't seem to be aware of her embarrassment.

'That wasn't what you thought the other night,' he reminded her wryly.

She flushed wildly, hating the way she was so vulnerable to the vivid mental images conjured up by his dry words.

'That was different,' she protested unwisely. 'You were——'

'Virtually naked?' he supplied for her.

'A stranger,' Harriet supplemented hurriedly.

'And now I'm not. I see. So it's not apprehension of the unpredictability of my sex as a whole that you objected to, but more specifically me, or rather my touch.'

Harriet stared at him, wondering how on earth they had managed to stray off the safe, distant conversation they had been sharing to this distinctly unsafe and dangerous one.

She suppressed an urgent need to touch her tongue to her lips to discover if they felt as hot and dry as they seemed.

'N—no such thing,' she managed to stammer, but he ignored her dazed protest.

Instead he said grimly, 'You really need have no fears, attractive though you undoubtedly are. I assure you that I am not in the habit of forcing uninvited attentions on your sex.'

Attractive, he had called her attractive! Harriet gaped at him, and then, while she was gathering her scattered wits, he was striding toward his Range Rover, leaving her staring after him like a tongue-tied fool.

Attractive... why on earth had he said that? He hadn't struck her as the kind of man to pay polite fictional compliments, just the reverse.

No matter how much she tried to dismiss it, the question kept returning to tease at her mind all through the evening, long after she had unpacked and put away her shopping, made her evening meal and settled down with a book which, when she had bought it, she had been sure would capture her attention to the exclusion of everything else.

CHAPTER FOUR

HARRIET woke up in the morning cautiously pleased to discover that she didn't now have any symptoms of the cold she had expected as a result of her soaking the previous day. The sneezes had been temporary effects.

It had stopped raining, but the sky was leaden. Autumn had arrived with a vengeance, and the brisk wind picked up the leaves from the trees, sending them whirling into drifting flurries.

Autumn: season of mellow fruitfulness, a time of nostalgia, a time haunted with prescient awareness of the winter to come. Perhaps it was the time of year that was responsible for all the odd things she was feeling, and not after all, as she had feared, Rigg.

It was a tempting line of thought, but a dangerous one. She had made up her mind last night that she was not going to allow herself to dwell on Rigg or her response to him any more. She had other things to do. Now was the time to give her thoughts a more sensible and productive direction before it was too late.

Too late for what? she mused uneasily as she had her breakfast. Too late to stop herself falling in love with him? She put down the toast that had suddenly lost its crisp, wholemeal flavour and turned to cardboard in her mouth.

Falling in love—at her age, and on the strength of two brief meetings? Impossible! She was supposed to be a mature adult, not a teenager.

A brisk walk, and then down to work. That was the way to banish these foolish and unwanted emotions that seemed to be dominating her new life.

When she got outside she was glad of the warmth of her thick duffel coat, even if its brilliant scarlet colour now seemed to be a rather childish gesture of defiance against the conventions that had always ruled her life. Perhaps that was the answer; perhaps emotionally she had reverted to the teenager she had never been allowed to be. The thought amused and relieved her enough to make her mouth curl into a warm smile.

She breathed in deeply, letting the clean, sharp air fill her lungs. This was luxury after London. A rabbit ran out of the undergrowth ahead of her, startling her for a moment and then making her think of Ben, Trixie's dog.

A dog. She had always liked animals; perhaps she ought to get a pet . . . Louise had been allergic to them, which had meant that when they were children animals could never be allowed in the house.

A dog. Yes, she would like that.

By the time she got back to the cottage, the temperature had dropped several degrees and the wind had picked up. The glazier she had telephoned that morning had promised to repair the roof-light as quickly as he could.

She made herself a cup of coffee, guiltily aware of her unhealthy enjoyment of its caffeine-induced addiction, and promising herself, as she did regularly, that she would switch to decaffeinated, knowing quite well that she most probably wouldn't.

It was sheer luxury then to sit down at her typewriter, without having to do so as though she were engaged in something underhand and secret.

Her writing had always been something she felt protective and defensive about, trying to snatch time out of her busy schedule to shut herself away in her own room to work.

Now her typewriter was firmly ensconced on the sturdy kitchen table she had bought specifically with her work in mind. When she lifted her head from the typewriter, she could look straight through the window and out into the wilderness of the garden beyond it.

Over a quick lunch of soup and a wholemeal roll she allowed herself to daydream about how the garden might look next summer. She was itching to get to grips with it. The garden in London had been small and very utilitarian. Selflessly she had given it over almost entirely to the children, believing that they needed it more than she did.

But here there was so much more scope. The cottage had almost an acre of land around it, part of which had apparently once been a well-tended vegetable plot which she hoped to resurrect. It was true that her experience of gardening was extremely limited, but she was enthusiastic and eager to learn. She daydreamed a little, trying to imagine how the unruly, dishevelled hedges would look once they were tamed and trimmed, and how the borders could be restored to order and filled with the kind of flowers so wonderfully portrayed in the paintings of Helen Allingham.

Scolding herself for wasting time daydreaming, Harriet turned her attention back to her work. Her publishers had approved her tentative outline for her new book, their approval giving her the confidence to allow her imagination a freer rein.

She was so engrossed in her work that she didn't realise she had a visitor until the kitchen door opened and Trixie walked in.

'Sorry,' she apologised with a smile, 'but I was knocking on the front door for ages, and I knew you must be here because your car's here. 'I've brought your things back,' she added, handing Harriet the bundle of clothes she was carrying. 'I would have come over sooner, but Rigg is such a fusspot.' She pulled a face. 'He said I should telephone first, in case you didn't want any visitors. Honestly, he's archaic sometimes in his attitude. Take his refusal to let me go away with Eva and her mother. He thinks that just because Mrs Soames likes to go out and enjoy herself she isn't responsible enough to look after us . . . Look after us! I'm eighteen—well, almost eighteen!'

Sensibly, Harriet forbore to point out that even almost eighteen-year-olds needed just as much, if not more, looking after than children.

'I wish you would speak to him,' Trixie told her, startling Harriet into staring at her.

'Me?'

'After all, you're a schoolteacher. He's got to admit that you know what you're talking about.'

Her assumption that Harriet must naturally be on her side made Harriet sigh a little for her youthful naïveté and confidence. No wonder Rigg was reluctant to let her go away under the care of a woman he plainly did not feel he could trust to take the responsibility seriously.

'I don't think your uncle's the kind of man who'd allow his own judgement to be swayed by anyone else,' she told Trixie firmly, steeling herself against the appeal in the girl's eyes, so like her uncle's.

'Oh, but he likes you... I can tell,' Trixie told her artlessly.

Trixie, Harriet suspected, saw what she wanted to see and wasn't above indulging in a little strategic manipulation when she thought it might suit her own ends.

'I can't say anything to your uncle,' Harriet told her firmly. 'Principally because, quite honestly, Trixie, from what you've told me, I think he has every reason to feel worried about allowing you to go on holiday with Mrs Soames.'

She saw the younger girl's face fall, and said more gently, 'Be honest with yourself. Surely you can understand how worried he must have been to discover that Mrs Soames had sent you home with a man Rigg doesn't know... a man, moreover, who had been drinking?'

There was a small pause, and then Trixie admitted honestly, 'Yes. I can see why he was cross, but if he'd let me explain properly——! Mrs Soames was late getting back because she'd been delayed by a client. She's an interior designer, and she can't afford to ignore possible business. And then when she got back she discovered that she'd only got enough petrol left to get to the garage in the morning, so when Maurice—her boyfriend—offered to give me a lift, it seemed the ideal solution.'

She sighed, and her lips twitched. 'Of course, it didn't help that Rigg had decided to drive over to Mrs Soames's house to pick me up himself, and that Maurice almost ran into him just outside the drive... He accused Maurice of driving while he'd had too much to drink. He was furious. Maurice is younger than Mrs Soames, and I think Rigg thought that he was going to try and make a pass at me... I'm sure he wasn't. I was so angry with Rigg—he made me look like a child and I'm *not*! That's why on Sunday I decided to teach him a lesson, to put *him* in a situation where people would make the wrong judgements about him so that *he* could see how he liked being made to look silly!'

She gave Harriet a mischievous look. 'He told me about how he mistook your car for mine. I bet he was furious. I'd love to have seen his face!'

'You wouldn't,' Harriet assured her decisively, and was then unable to resist asking, 'How on earth did you persuade him to strip off and jump in the river in the first place?'

Trixie grinned at her.

'Oh, that bit was easy. He hates being driven by anyone, so he was sitting with his eyes closed, and I simply pulled up and screamed to him that I'd seen someone struggling in the water. He didn't hesitate. I knew he wouldn't,' she said smugly.

Harriet wondered if she knew just how lucky she was to have someone in her life who was so deeply caring and responsible.

'As soon as he jumped in the river, I drove off... I must admit I thought it would be someone local who would find him. I never thought of it being a stranger.' She laughed again. 'Did you *really* think he might be a rapist? He was furious about that!'

'I can well imagine,' Harriet told her drily, the lecture she was about to deliver forestalled by the sound of a car pulling up outside.

This time she did hear the front doorbell, and found when she went to open the door that Trixie had come with her.

The woman outside was obviously well known to Trixie, because she greeted her with a warm smile.

'I'm Nora Fellows, the Vicar's wife,' her visitor introduced herself as Harriet invited her in.

'I heard in the village that you'd moved in. We're only a small community here and rather far-flung, so we try to keep in touch with one another as much as possible, but if you'd prefer to be left alone, please don't be afraid of saying so. Small communities can seem a little claustrophobic at times. On this occasion, though, my visit does have a purpose. It's my husband's sixtieth birthday this week, and we're having a large party at the Vicarage to celebrate it. All the village is invited, and of course that includes you. Rather short notice, I know.'

Touched by her warmth and kindness, Harriet thanked her and readily accepted her invitation, which was for Saturday afternoon, it seemed.

'They've had a collection in the village to buy him a present,' Trixie advised after Mrs Fellows had left. Harriet made a mental note to make enquiries at the post office to see if it was too late for her to subscribe to the community present.

'What are you typing?' Trixie asked next, perching on the kitchen table and absently removing an apple from the bowl.

She was as friendly as a puppy and just as vulnerable, Harriet reflected. No wonder Rigg felt she was in need of the protection of an adult more cautious and concerned than Mrs Soames appeared to be.

'I'm writing a book,' Harriet told her, and was a little overwhelmed by Trixie's awed reception of the information.

'You're a *writer*... I'd love to write,' she said dreamily. 'But I thought you said you were a teacher.'

'Yes, I am... or rather I was,' Harriet agreed. Then she added firmly, 'And if I don't get back to work, I suspect I'll find my new career as a writer will be a very short one indeed.'

Cheerfully, Trixie took the hint, removing herself from her perch on the table and heading for the back door, where she paused.

'Shall I tell Rigg that you're OK then?'

'Yes, please,' Harriet responded, adding. 'I've still got the clothes you loaned me. I'll wash them and get them back to you just as soon as I can.'

'No sweat,' Trixie told her with a grin, as she disappeared through the door.

What a very contradictory man Rigg Matthews was, Harriet reflected an hour later, finally admitting that Trixie's visit had totally broken her concentration on her work. On the one hand he was so austere, so remote and distant, and she could have sworn in addition that he almost actively disliked her, and yet he had taken the trouble to send Trixie over to make sure she was all right.

Genuine concern for her? Hardly. Much more likely that his enquiry was prompted by the deep vein of responsibility she had seen so clearly in his concern for his young niece.

It was plain to Harriet that no matter how much Trixie might rebel against his authority she obviously loved and trusted him a great deal.

She wondered idly if the girl who had left him at the altar had ever regretted her decision. She found it very hard to imagine what kind of woman would turn her back on a man like Rigg.

Stop it, she berated herself as she made a fresh jug of coffee. If you don't want to find yourself back in front of a classroom full of twelve-year-olds you'd better get down to some work.

The rest of the week passed quietly and productively. Harriet had one visit from Trixie, to whom she returned her now clean clothes with grateful thanks.

It was obvious to her that Trixie was lonely and, more, that she was looking for adult support in her campaign to persuade Rigg to allow her to go skiing with her friend and her mother. But from what Trixie had let slip to Harriet about Mrs Soames's lifestyle, she felt more inclined to support Rigg's decision than to oppose it.

As gently as she could, she explained to Trixie why she felt Rigg's decision was the right one.

'But I'll soon be eighteen,' Trixie protested. 'Just because Eva's mother has lots of boyfriends and things, it doesn't mean that I'm going to copy her.

I am capable of making my own decisions about how I want to live,' she added, with more than a little touch of her uncle's hauteur and stubbornness.

'Of course you are,' Harriet agreed, and then added quietly, 'But sometimes, no matter how adult we consider ourselves, we can get drawn into situations we don't want, because we don't have the experience to deal with them.'

Trixie was an intelligent girl, and Harriet could see her almost visibly digesting her comment.

'You mean like having to have a lift with Maurice, even though I'd much rather have rung Rigg and asked him to collect me?'

'Mmm,' Harriet agreed, waiting.

'Well, I didn't really want Maurice to drive me home.' She pulled a face. 'There's something about him. I can't describe it, he's just—well, a bit creepy, if you know what I mean, but there was no need for Rigg to carry on the way he did. Making me look a complete fool . . . Eva said Maurice and her mother laughed their heads off later at him. Eva says he's unbelievably archaic.'

'Eva says?' Harriet asked, lifting her eyebrows a little. 'And what does Trixie say? It's your own judgement of people and situations that matters most, Trixie, or at least it should be. Rigg might seem to be a mite autocratic to you now, but, believe me, he only wants what's best for you.'

She saw the face Trixie pulled and told her, 'No, I'm not part of an adult conspiracy against anyone in their teens. If I thought he was being unduly strict I'd tell you so, but think about it, Trixie. You're obviously not entirely happy yourself with Eva's mother's lifestyle.'

'No,' Trixie agreed, a little reluctantly. 'But just because of that, it doesn't mean that Eva and I shouldn't be friends. They only moved up here a few months ago, and Eva doesn't have many friends. Besides,' she added wistfully, 'I've always wanted to go skiing. Rigg used to go every winter before my folks were killed. He was with them— or at least he would have been, only he didn't go out that day because he was expecting an important phone call... They were skiing off piste and there was an avalanche.'

Instinctively Harriet reached out to cover the younger girl's hands with her own.

'It must have been awful for you,' she commiserated.

'It was, but it was even worse for Rigg... He had to identify them and everything. I do love him.' She got up and moved restlessly around the kitchen. 'But he has to go away quite a lot. Mrs Arkwright's OK, but sometimes I wish that Rigg were married. I'd like to have some cousins... an aunt.'

They were treading on dangerous ground now, and instinctively Harriet knew how much Rigg would resent an intrusion into his privacy in the shape of any confidences Trixie might unwittingly make to her.

To try and head her off, she said quickly, 'Well, your uncle isn't exactly in his dotage. He may well marry.'

But it was the wrong thing to say, because immediately Trixie pounced on her comment with a vigorous denial.

'No...no, he won't. When Gemma walked out on him, it broke his heart, and he swore then that he'd never trust another woman.'

Harriet blinked a little. Such vehement emotionalism seemed totally at odds with the cool, contained man she had seen.

'It was before I was born, just after Mum and Dad were married. Mum told me all about it,' Trixie hurried on, ignoring Harriet's attempts to stop her.

'Gemma was a model and he fell madly in love with her. They were all living in London then. Mum and Dad were newly married, and Rigg was just down from university. Mum said that Gemma was stunningly beautiful outwardly, but inwardly... I think she was quite glad really that they didn't get married. Rigg didn't have much money in those days. He told Mum and Dad that he and Gemma were going to be married, and then, just days before the wedding, he went round to see them and told them that it was all off and that Gemma was marrying someone else. Someone she'd met through her modelling...a lot older than Rigg and with tons of money.'

She pulled another face. 'Mum said that Rigg was devastated. I think it's awfully romantic, don't you?'

Romantic?

'No, I don't,' Harriet refuted crisply. 'If you want my opinion I think your uncle had a lucky escape. If he had married this Gemma, he'd have probably been thoroughly miserable.'

Trixie frowned at her.

'Have you ever been in love, Harriet?' she asked her curiously. 'I mean really, madly, passionately in love.'

'No,' Harriet admitted shortly. She didn't want to reveal to Trixie the shortcomings in her nature, or to admit that she was not the kind of woman to inspire deep passionate emotion in a man.

'I'm not going to fall in love until I'm at least thirty,' Trixie told her importantly. 'I don't think any woman should commit herself to a man until she's done something with her life, do you?' she enquired.

'I certainly don't think it's a good idea for anyone, man or woman, to commit themselves to a long-term relationship before they've got a reasonable amount of self-knowledge,' Harriet agreed cautiously.

'Well, what I want to do is to establish myself in my career,' Trixie told her weightily. 'After all, a woman needs to be sure that she can support herself financially these days, instead of relying on someone else to support her, don't you agree?'

'I think it's sensible for a woman to be able to support herself if necessary,' Harriet agreed.

'Will you ever get married?' Trixie asked her, catching her off guard with the swift change of subject.

'I shouldn't expect so,' Harriet answered her honestly. She did not go on to admit that the trouble was that, although she was now of an age when a comfortable marriage to someone of similar tastes and ideals should be more important to her than passion and intensity, there was a small, rebellious part of her that yearned for the latter and that said that if she were never going to experience it then she might as well stay single.

After Trixie had gone, she returned to her work, but snippets of their conversation kept floating back into her mind. She acknowledged that they were forming as yet almost nebulous strands of thoughts that were edging her away from her present work, and inciting her to try something different.

Adult fiction?

Too ambitious? Possibly, but the challenge of it was already exciting her imagination.

Autumn was now taking a firm grip on the countryside; the gales Rigg had warned were imminent arrived in the early hours of Friday morning battering at the cottage's doors and windows, waking her up to lie snug and warm beneath the heaped covers of the large old-fashioned bed she had now acquired. There was an unfamiliar, almost childish pleasure to be found in lying there, safe and warm, while outside the gale howled and tore at the world with angry fingers.

She had looked forward to her move out of London, but she had not realised how much pleasure it was going to give her. Already, despite the self-induced pressure caused by her work, she felt healthier, happier than she had done in years. She could well understand why Rigg had moved his business from London up here to the Borders.

Rigg. The one serpent in her new Eden. Or, rather, it was her own traitorous habit of allowing him to constantly invade her thoughts that was the one serpent in her new-found paradise.

On Friday morning she walked down to the village to buy some stamps. The postmistress

greeted her by name. Harriet had gone down earlier
in the week to introduce herself, and now made enquiries about the collection for the Vicar's birthday
present.

Her enquiry produced an approving smile and
the information that she was just in time to
contribute.

'What the Vicar really wants is a computer. Not
that he knows we're getting him one,' she added
with a chuckle, 'and we certainly couldn't have af-
forded it without Rigg's help. He's even arranged
for the Vicar to go on a familiarisation course for
it, whatever that might be ... So you'll be going to
the party then?' she asked.

Harriet nodded. Louise would have scoffed at
the pleasure it gave her to be included in the life of
the village like this. The kind of parties her sister
liked were held at glamorous locations and filled
with expensively dressed, well-known people.

Their tastes had always been so different. She had
written to Louise twice since her marriage, but as
yet had received no letter back. She felt she ought
to have missed her sister and the twins more than
she actually was doing, but Trixie's visits gave her
far more pleasure than she had ever found in her
sister's company.

Trixie had confided in her that she was hoping
to go on to university when she left school, but that
she wasn't quite sure yet what course she wanted
to take.

Rigg had done a far better job in guiding Trixie
towards maturity than she had managed with
Louise, Harriet thought.

She walked back to the cottage, enjoying the blustering wind, noting the subtle changes in the landscape that warned that winter was not far away.

In the village they were building a large communal bonfire for the Fifth of November. Tickets for it were on sale at the post office, and on impulse she bought one.

You never knew, she might find some inspiration there for her work.

The brisk walk seemed to have activated her imagination and she worked hard all afternoon, forced to stop typing when her aching wrists told her how long she had been working.

While she was in the post office, she had bought herself a couple of glossy magazines, and she spent the evening leafing through them.

Although all the basic work had been done on the cottage, there was still a good deal of room for improvement where the décor was concerned.

The glossy, too perfect room sets featured in the magazines weren't what she had in mind. She closed her eyes, picturing her small sitting-room comfortably furnished with the kind of sofas that subtly encouraged relaxation. The room faced north, and needed rich warm colours, rusts and terracottas. Mentally furnishing and redecorating the room behind her closed eyelids, she was infuriated when, out of nowhere, Rigg's imposing form took shape on one of her sofas... Exasperated, she opened her eyes. What on earth was the matter with her, indulging in these stupid fantasies?

Didn't she have enough to occupy her mind? Was that why it kept slipping treacherously into these ridiculous daydreams?

Thoroughly annoyed with herself, she got up. In the old days, when Louise and the twins had got too much for her, she had found some relief from her emotions in a task such as scrubbing the kitchen floor.

Perhaps it would be equally effective in banishing Rigg from her thoughts.

Half an hour later, the kitchen floor was spanking clean, and she told herself severely that these idiotic yearnings had to stop. If she had to start mooning about over some unobtainable man at the supposedly mature age of thirty-four, why on earth did she have to pick on a man like Rigg?

Why? Did she really need to ask herself that question? No woman seeing Rigg as she had seen him on that first occasion could remain immune to his maleness. In the past very male men had been a species she had always found slightly intimidating. Rigg didn't intimidate her. He fascinated, compelled, infuriated and absorbed her; and the more she learned about him through Trixie's artless confidences, the more that absorption grew.

So often her mind would trick her, slipping sideways into contemplation of him, as though pulled there relentlessly by a deep, hidden current. Too often, but not any more. The danger signs were written there clearly enough for anyone to read; she'd be a fool to ignore them. Rigg had no interest in her, and even if he had... She walked restlessly around her kitchen, resisting the temptation to imagine what it would be like to be desired... wanted... loved by a man like Rigg.

That night, for the first time since her arrival, she slept badly, her sleep interrupted by deep and dangerous dreams from which her conscious mind dutifully wrested her.

On Saturday morning she woke up feeling drained and irritable. The phone rang while she was unenthusiastically forcing herself to eat an unwanted breakfast.

Half expecting it to be Trixie, Harriet froze when she heard a familiar male voice saying crisply, 'Harriet, it's Rigg here. I believe you're going to the Vicar's birthday do this afternoon. Mrs Fellows has asked us to give you a lift. They're very short of parking space at the Vicarage, so it makes sense for as many people to travel together as possible. Had you any time in mind for setting out?'

It took her several valuable seconds to pull her scattered wits together. The shock of the disorientating sound of his voice, so close on the heels of last night's disturbing dreams, the sensations its slightly acerbic and very male reverberations produced in her body, the thrilling heady pleasure of knowing that she was going to see him, followed by the stark acknowledgement that their meeting was not at any instigation of his, all held her silent. Her see-sawing emotions, and the sheer futility and stupidity of what she was allowing herself to feel made it impossible to reply to him immediately.

'Harriet? Are you there?'

'Yes,' she told him faintly, and then pulled herself together enough to say with some modicum of calmness, 'I didn't have any particular time in mind. I'm quite happy to fit in with you.'

Had he not added that rider about the shortage of car parking space, she must have refused his offer, coming as it did at someone else's suggestion.

She might have fallen crazily, idiotically in love with him like the fool she was, but no one but her was going to know about it. She had her pride, after all. And that was all she did have to stand between her and the appalling probability that she might make a complete fool of herself.

Pride... wasn't it supposed to be a vice, not a virtue?

'Well, in that case, should we say three-thirty?' she heard Rigg say briefly.

'I'll be ready,' she assured him.

When she replaced the receiver, she found that she was clutching it so tightly that her fingers were white. At seventeen Trixie possessed more sang-froid and sophistication than she did. Perhaps it was her age, she agonised, as she threw away the breakfast that her now churning stomach could not possibly tolerate.

Her age—yes, that must be the answer, she decided desperately as she automatically poured herself a fresh mug of coffee. She was going through some sort of odd mid-life crisis—some sort of emotional attempt to experience now what she had not experienced in her real youth.

Feeling slightly better now that she had found some sort of explanation for her totally unfamiliar feelings, she went upstairs to put on her coat.

She ought to have driven into Hawick to do her shopping yesterday but she had never got round to it. Now she would have to do it today.

The wind had dropped, leaving the sky swept clean of clouds, and a pale, cold shade of blue from which sharp sunlight spilled, turning the leaves and foliage into a rainbow of russets and golds.

Hawick was busy, but she was lucky enough to find a spot to park.

Shopping here was a much more leisurely affair than it had been in London. Even in the supermarket the girls on the tills seemed to know the names of their customers and exchanged a few friendly words with them. The soft Borders accent fell pleasantly on her ears, restful and gentle.

She walked slowly back to her car, enjoying the sunshine and the busy bustle of the other shoppers. As she turned a corner, the display in the window of a small dress shop caught her eye, and she went across to admire the bright scarlet knitted two-piece. The top was long, just allowing a few inches of the short, straight, matching skirt to show beneath it. The scarlet wool was knitted in an attractive chunky cable design, with a broad scarlet stripe of satin ribbon running from shoulder to hem down the front.

There was something richly appealing about the outfit, and while Harriet was admiring it another older woman came to stand beside her and admire it as well.

'It's lovely, isn't it?' she commented warmly, with the same friendliness that Harriet had already experienced from other locals. 'Jan always has marvellous clothes, but I must admit that outfit's in a class of its own. Lucky you, you've got exactly the right colour to show it off... and the right figure,' she sighed, glancing wryly at her own pleasantly plump form.

With another smile, she went on her way, while Harriet hesitated outside the shop. She had no need of any more clothes, and the outfit would be ex-

pensive, she guessed. She hadn't even been thinking
of buying it until the other woman had put the idea
in her mind. It wasn't the sort of thing she wore at
all, and yet somehow or other she was inside the
shop and a pretty fair-haired woman of her own
age was coming forward to help her.

'The outfit in the window? It's the only one we've
got, I'm afraid, and a very small size.' She looked
judiciously at Harriet and then added, 'I don't
know, though. You are only small, aren't you?'

Her duffel coat added bulk as well as warmth,
and when Harriet took it off the other woman's
eyes lightened.

'Oh, yes, it should fit you perfectly!' she ex-
claimed, and before Harriet could protest she was
removing the outfit from the window and
shepherding Harriet into a comfortable fitting-room
to try it on.

It did fit perfectly, Harriet acknowledged as she
studied her reflection in the mirror. The colour
lifted her pale skin and added extra rich tones to
her hair. Moreover, there was something very appealing about the combination of the high-necked
generous top and the narrow slim skirt.

It wasn't an over-provocative outfit, and
yet...and yet there was something about it that
would guarantee its wearer a second look, Harriet
decided.

Ignoring the cold voice of reason that warned
her that she was behaving in the most foolish way
possible, she changed back into her own clothes
and, before she could resist the impulse, told the
other woman that she wanted to buy it.

It was every bit as expensive as she had anticipated, but a justifiable expense, surely? She had
very few clothes she could socialise in. Assuring
herself firmly that she had not bought it simply so
that Rigg could see her in it, she headed back to
her car. She had spent longer in Hawick than she
had intended. She hummed in tune with the radio
as she drove homewards, refusing to admit that her
good spirits had any connection whatsoever with
the fact that she was going to see Rigg.

CHAPTER FIVE

By THREE o'clock Harriet was dressed and ready, her stomach fluttering nervously with tension. She had washed and brushed her hair into a soft bob, and the reflection thrown back at her by her mirror was a startlingly different one from her old London image. Was it just wishful thinking that she looked younger—softer somehow?

Giving herself a mental shake for her foolishness, she went downstairs.

The card she had bought and written was on the table with her bag. She checked that her keys were in the door; she suspected that Rigg was not a man who would appreciate being kept waiting.

When half-past three came and went without his appearance her tension increased. At twenty to four she was just debating whether or not she ought to telephone the Hall, when Trixie's red VW came racing up her drive.

While she watched Trixie got out and came hurrying to the door.

Schooling her features to conceal the sick disappointment churning through her, Harriet opened the door to her.

'Sorry I'm late,' Trixie apologised. 'Rigg can't make it, by the way,' she added, as Harriet locked up and followed her back to her car. 'Some crisis or other at the factory.'

As she got into the car and fastened her seatbelt, Harriet hoped profoundly that nothing of what she was feeling showed in her face or voice. Deliberately she didn't allow herself the luxury of asking whether or not Rigg was likely to appear at the party. It was her own fault that she felt like this, she derided herself as Trixie chattered blithely to her. She had warned herself against the folly of letting herself dream stupid daydreams. Rigg had no interest in her, none whatsoever.

'Rigg said to give you his apologies,' Trixie told her, changing gear with a flair that Harriet half envied.

She was a good driver, confident and careful, but then of course Rigg would never have allowed her out on the roads in charge of a car if he was not sure she had sufficient skill, despite Trixie's earlier comment about his keeping his eyes closed when she drove. Rigg. Rigg! Her stomach jolted ferociously, and she closed her eyes.

'Are you all right?' Trixie asked her anxiously. 'You look awfully pale.'

'I'm fine,' Harriet lied wanly.

'I like your outfit, by the way,' Trixie told her. 'That colour's stunning on you. I'd love to be able to wear red, but with my hair! Back to school on Monday,' she sighed with mock horror. 'At least they don't make us wear a uniform in the sixth.'

Somehow or other Harriet managed to force herself to respond to Trixie's chatter, and they were soon pulling into the Vicarage's overgrown drive, to join the other cars already parked there.

'The Vicar's great,' Trixie told her unexpectedly as they walked to the door. 'A bit sort of absent-minded at times, but not at all religious, if you know what I mean.'

Harriet couldn't help grinning a little at her description, and it was while she was standing with her mouth curling into a warm smile, her bright red outfit a glowing splash of colour against the greyness of the stone-built Vicarage, that the door opened and the man standing just inside saw her.

His eyes narrowed appreciatively, a gleam of interest lightening their dark brown depths as he smiled at Harriet and then said, 'Hello, Trixie. No Rigg? Never mind. Come on in . . . *after* you've introduced me to your friend.'

A swift glance of comprehension crossed Trixie's face.

'Harriet, this is Dan, the Vicar's son. Dan, this is Harriet, our new neighbour.'

'A new neighbour? Excellent . . . so I won't be poaching on Rigg's territory if I steal you away then, will I, Harriet?'

He was a little younger than herself, Harriet judged, an attractive self-confident man, who she suspected was well versed in the vulnerabilities of her sex. Had she met him in London she would have felt overwhelmed by him, tongue-tied and nervous, and yet now, apart from noting absently that physically he was attractive, if somewhat boyish for a man in his early thirties, she felt nothing whatsoever, as he flattered her outrageously and insisted on escorting her personally to introduce her to his father.

The Vicar greeted them warmly, and Harriet could see why Trixie liked him. He had a gentleness of spirit you couldn't help warming to. She wondered briefly how such an unworldly couple had managed to produce such a very worldly son.

He went to get both her and Trixie a drink, and while he was gone Trixie told her rather curtly, 'Dan lectures at Newcastle University. Mrs Fellows is always saying she wishes he'd get married, but Rigg says he enjoys teaching his students to fall in love with him too much to settle for one woman. He really fancies you,' she added.

Harriet smiled at her.

'I think that's just his manner. After all, if his tastes run to students, he's hardly likely to be interested in me, is he?'

For some reason Trixie didn't seem to approve of the fact that Dan was showing an interest in her. Personally, Harriet suspected he was the kind of man who would flirt with any woman, almost automatically. Listening to him with half her attention while he complimented and flattered her, she studied Trixie, relieved to see that it wasn't any personal interest in him that was bringing the frown of disapproval to Trixie's eyes.

As the afternoon progressed and both of them clung to her, almost like two dogs with a bone, her amusement gave way to exasperation. She was sure that Dan was deliberately baiting Trixie, although for what purpose she wasn't entirely sure. Trixie, it was obvious, was not going to leave her alone with Dan, and Dan, for some reason of his own, was doing everything he could to get rid of the younger girl.

Deciding that she had had enough, Harriet was just about to suggest to Trixie that it might be a good idea if they left, when the Vicar's wife came up to them and asked Trixie if she would give her a hand collecting empty plates and glasses.

With the good manners that Harriet had already noted, Trixie allowed herself to be drawn away, albeit after giving Dan a dark glower.

'Thanks, Ma,' Dan drawled outrageously when they were both out of earshot. 'And now that we've got rid of your own personal limpet, what did Rigg do? Set her to guard you?'

'Rigg?' Harriet stared at him, colour rising swiftly up under her skin. 'You were deliberately baiting her,' she told him flatly. 'You can't blame her for responding...'

'Or guarding her uncle's personal and private property?' he suggested provocatively.

Harriet felt her colour deepen. Her face was burning with embarrassment and anger.

'You're leaping to unwarranted conclusions,' she told him sharply. 'Rigg is my neighbour, that's all. I am most definitely not his or any other man's property.'

The anger in her eyes showed him what she thought of his overtly sexist remark. How could any man in this day and age, never mind one who apparently tutored young people, have dared to suggest that a woman was a piece of property?

She looked sharply at him, suspecting him of teasing her the same way he had been teasing Trixie, but he wasn't looking at her. Instead he was staring beyond her shoulder, a thoughtful expression on his face.

'I think you're lying to me,' he told her. 'If there's nothing between the two of you, why on earth is

Rigg glaring at me as though he'd like to ram a knife between my ribs?'

Rigg...here... Her heart swung crazily like a yoyo and she only just managed to stop herself from turning round. Instinctively she dropped her eyelids to conceal her expression from the man watching her.

Shrugging her shoulders, she said huskily, 'You're imagining things. Rigg has no interest in me.'

'Good. Prove it...have dinner with me tomorrow night.'

Have dinner with him. Her mouth dropped open, and she glanced distractedly round the room, assuring herself that she wasn't the only female here under the age of fifty and above the age of consent, to explain away his interest in her. She wasn't. She closed her mouth and stared at him.

Have dinner with him... While she was still assimilating his invitation she saw him smiling and heard him saying cheerfully, 'Hello there, Rigg. You made it, after all. I've just been persuading your delightful new neighbour to have dinner with me.'

Without turning round, Harriet could sense the coldness emanating from the man standing behind her. She was dismayingly conscious of having somehow or other won his disapproval. Was it because she wasn't with Trixie? But surely the girl was safe enough here in this very respectable gathering of people?

'Drinks are in the dining-room,' Dan was saying to Rigg.

'Unfortunately I can't stay. I only called in to wish your father a happy birthday. Trixie has school on Monday so I think I'll collect her and then we'll both leave.'

They would leave . . . What about her? Harriet wondered angrily, or had he forgotten that she had come with Trixie?

As calmly as she could, she turned round to face him and said evenly, 'I'd better say my goodbyes as well, then.'

'You're leaving?' Dan was frowning at her, patently not pleased.

'I came with Trixie,' she told him half absently. 'Naturally——'

'Well, I can give you a lift back.'

There was a full glass of wine in his hand and she had no way of knowing how much he had already drunk or how much he would continue to drink. She smiled firmly at him and shook her head.

'No. It's a kind thought, but I wouldn't want to disrupt the party.' Conscious of Rigg's austere, silent presence, she turned to go, but Dan reached for her hand and held on to it as she tried to tug it away.

'Don't forget that we have a date tomorrow evening, will you?' he said softly. 'I'll pick you up at seven-thirty, shall I?'

Not wanting to refuse him in front of Rigg, Harriet gave him a brief smile and said nothing. She could already sense Rigg's impatience to be gone, and by the time she had removed her fingers from Dan's grip Rigg already had his back to her and was moving purposefully through the throng towards the Vicar and his wife.

'Rigg, nice to see you.' The Vicar smiled.

'A brief visit, I'm afraid.'

They exchanged civilities while Harriet stood to one side, trying to spot Trixie. She saw her at the same moment as Trixie saw them. The relief that flooded the younger girl's face when she caught sight of them surprised her a little.

In no time at all Trixie had made her way to Rigg's side. She seemed quite happy to leave, tucking one hand through Rigg's arm, and then holding on to Harriet with the other, so that the three of them were linked together.

Outside the temperature had dropped, frost already riming the hedges. The sky was clear, glittering brilliantly with stars, the air pure and still. Harriet breathed deeply, savouring it, and then shivered as the chill struck her skin.

She heard the familiar rattle of the VW's engine and turned to walk towards it, but to her astonishment the small car was already scooting down the drive.

Stunned, she stared after it.

'It's all right,' Rigg told her laconically, coming to stand beside her. 'I told Trixie I'd drop you off.'

Too bemused to ask him why, Harriet stared dumbly at him.

His breath was making small clouds of vapour on the cold air; a fresh breeze made her shiver involuntarily. She hadn't brought a jacket with her.

Watching her with a frown, Rigg moved between her and the chilly wind. His lean body provided a comforting windbreak, but he was standing far too close to her, Harriet recognised, as a tremor that had nothing to do with the cold chased over her skin. She only hoped that Rigg wouldn't recognise her second reaction for what it was.

'I'm afraid I had to leave the Range Rover out on the main road. Can you walk, or would you prefer...?'

He was glancing down doubtfully at her high-heeled shoes, and, remembering the state of the Vicarage drive, Harriet could understand his doubts.

'I can walk,' she told him sturdily. At least walking the length of the drive would keep her warmer than standing here waiting for Rigg to bring the Range Rover.

She turned determinedly away from him and set off down the drive as she spoke to prove she meant what she said, but what she hadn't anticipated was that Rigg would catch up with her in a couple of quick strides and take hold of her arm. Automatically he was drawing her against the protection of his body, not in any sensual way, but more as he might have taken hold of Trixie, she recognised, gritting her teeth against her own foolish reaction to his closeness.

She was concentrating so hard on ignoring the signals her body was sending to her brain, and her intense awareness of him, that she forgot to watch where she was walking, with the result that she stepped right into a deep water-filled rut in the drive.

The shock of the cold water on her feet made her gasp as Rigg tightened his grip on her arm to stop her from stumbling.

'Are you all right?'

The brilliance of the stars gave plenty of light for her to see the way he was frowning down at her, and more than enough light for her to have seen the puddle and avoided it. Her face hot with guilt-induced embarrassment, she half turned away from him, wanting to avoid the searching intentness of his scrutiny.

'Fine,' she told him shortly. 'Stupid of me; I wasn't looking where I was going.'

'No doubt you had other things on your mind,' he agreed curtly.

Immediately Harriet tensed and looked at him, her heart doing somersaults inside her. Surely he hadn't *guessed*...didn't *know*...but his next words set her mind at rest.

'Well, unless you want to go on your dinner date tomorrow evening with a sprained ankle, I suggest that you concentrate on looking where you're going and not on Dan.'

Relief overwhelmed her, quickly followed by anger. He was treating her as though she were a brainless child. Her mouth firmed as she suppressed an instinctive urge to tell him to go on without her and she would find her own way home, but the end of the drive was already in sight and, with it, the familiar shape of his dark blue Range Rover.

Her feet were squelching uncomfortably in what had been a very expensive pair of court shoes. She doubted that they would survive their immersion in the icy cold puddle and told herself it served her right for being so stupid.

One thing she couldn't fault Rigg on was his manners, she acknowledged as he unlocked the passenger door for her. He was parked at a slight angle and as she measured the distance up into the seat she wished she weren't wearing such a short straight skirt.

She hoped Rigg would go and unlock the driver's door so that he wouldn't witness what she suspected would be an undignified scramble into the seat, but it seemed he had already recognised her difficulty.

Before she could attempt to move, he said brusquely, 'I think it will be easier if I lift you in.'

Before she could think of objecting, he was picking her up in a determined and asexual hold, his hands resting firmly either side of her waist and up over her lower ribcage.

She prayed that he couldn't measure the frantic thud of her heartbeat, or that if he did he would not realise what was causing it.

She was a slim woman, but practical enough always to be amused by the screen antics of heroes who gallantly swept their heroines up in their arms without any apparent alteration in their breathing. Modern women were too sensible to think of themselves as delicate, feather-light creatures to be swept off their feet by strong, virile men, and so she was astonished by the ease with which Rigg did pick her up. True, there was nothing remotely loverlike or romantic in his manner towards her, but there was an unexpected ease in his movements that left her feeling oddly breathless and weak.

As he deposited her in the seat, one of her shoes fell off.

'Your feet are soaking.'

He made it sound an accusation.

'Yes,' Harriet agreed drily. 'It does tend to happen when you go paddling about in puddles without wellingtons.'

She saw that he was smiling faintly. Smiling at *her*...the tug of sensation on her heartstrings was surely completely out of proportion to what was after all no more than a brief acknowledgement of her remark.

'As soon as we get going I'll turn on the heater. That should dry your feet out at least. It won't dry your shoes, though. You'd better take them off,' he instructed her as he released her and turned to walk round to the driver's door.

She felt chilled and bereft without the warm, sure touch of his hands, and treacherously into her thoughts slid a dangerous curiosity to know what it would be like to have his hands on her bare skin, not as an impatient and distant male wanting to accomplish a set task, but as a lover.

Angrily she pushed the undermining, persuasive thoughts away and tried to concentrate on more mundane things, such as telephoning the Vicarage in the morning and cancelling her date with Dan. He was an attractive man, a man used to female admiration, but he had no appeal for her. She wanted to spend the day studying her living-room, and deciding on how she was going to decorate it.

Decorating had been a necessity in the days when she was having to support Louise and the twins, and she had found that after her first bungled attempts to hang wallpaper and paint doors she rather enjoyed the sense of achievement such work brought her.

The cottage had two quite deep alcoves, either side of the chimney breast, and she wanted to find someone locally who could build cupboards in these alcoves for her. Once that was done, she would try her hand at painting them herself.

Now that the Range Rover was in motion she was beginning to feel the warmth from its powerful heater. She wiggled her toes luxuriously in the hot air. Although the cottage had open fires both in the sitting-room and in her bedroom, which she had elected to retain, she had also had central heating installed, and tonight she was going to be glad of it.

A sharp sickle moon had risen to the brilliant cold light reflected from the stars, showing quite plainly the heavy riming of frost on the hedgerows and the fields beyond them.

She glanced at Rigg, noting the confident, steady way he held the steering-wheel, knowing that he was a driver she need have no fears would take any unnecessary risks.

A misogynist, Trixie had called him. Had there really been no women in his life since his bride walked out on him? It seemed unlikely. Despite his coolness towards her, Harriet suspected that he was a man who was capable of very intense passion indeed, but perhaps he would deliberately choose to keep that side of his life hidden from the young and impressionable teenage girl under his care. Why, after all, should he *want* to marry? He wouldn't be the only man to prefer variety in his life, and he was certainly wealthy enough to indulge himself in whatever pleasures he chose to enjoy.

They were through the village now and approaching the turn-off to her drive. The muddy ruts at the entrance to it were now frozen ridges. The security lights she had installed came on as Rigg pulled up outside the front door.

It was only politeness, of course, that made him come round and open her door for her. She was wearing her damp and uncomfortable shoes, and this time there was no need for him to lift her. She bit her lip in vexation as she recognised how much she would have liked him to do so.

She was like a teenager obsessed by the image of some far distant idol, she told herself acidly, knowing even as the thought formed that it wasn't true. She *was* coming to know Rigg—to be aware of things about him—in a way that she had never known any other member of his sex; and the more she knew, the more she loved.

Loved... Such a small word to describe the enormity and complexity of all that she felt for him.

She thanked him without looking at him, found her keys and started to walk away until he stopped her. His hand was on her arm, drawing her back towards him.

'I almost forgot,' he told her. 'It's Trixie's birthday next week, and by tradition we always go out for dinner. This year she'd like you to join us. That is, if you're free?'

Harriet was stunned. She suspected from his expression that her company on such an occasion was the last thing he wanted.

The words of polite refusal were hovering on her tongue when he surprised her by adding, 'It would mean a lot to Trixie if you could come. She's become very attached to you.'

'But surely her friend, Eva Soames——' Harriet protested, and saw Rigg's mouth harden a fraction.

'Not her scene, I suspect ... Eva is a very sophisticated young woman; discos are much more her idea of a good time.'

She wanted to refuse, and yet how could she without hurting Trixie? That was the last thing she wanted to do.

'Well, if it's what Trixie wants,' she said uncertainly.

'It is.'

He seemed about to walk away, but then he hesitated, and said quietly, 'I believe I owe you some thanks, by the way.'

Harriet wasn't sure what he meant, and frowned.

'For supporting my refusal to allow Trixie to go away on holiday with Eva Soames and her mother.'

Harriet shrugged, a little awkwardly, wondering if he thought she was trying to curry favour with him through Trixie, and then told herself she was being hypersensitive. She might have been idiotic enough to have fallen in love with him, but no matter what she felt about him, those feelings would not alter her views on other matters, even if those views clashed with his.

'From what Trixie has told me about Mrs Soames, I could understand your reluctance to entrust Trixie to her care, but you can't shelter Trixie from everything all her life.'

'Is that what you think I'm trying to do?' He grimaced a little. 'Perhaps I am a little overprotective, but it's a heavy responsibility becoming father to a teenage girl overnight, so to speak.' He shot Harriet an enquiring look. 'She's told you about her parents' deaths, has she?'

'Yes,' Harriet confirmed. 'She's obviously come to terms with it marvellously. She's been lucky to have someone on hand to take care of her. That must have lessened the intensity of the tragedy a little.'

'We've always got on very well. Robert, my brother, was ten years older than me, and we were involved in a similar situation ourselves. Our parents died while I was at university—a car accident. Robert was just about to get married to Jen. After the estate was settled it was discovered that there wasn't as much money as we'd always thought. It could have meant my leaving university, but Robert insisted that I stay on. What's more, he and Jen not only supported me financially through those years, but they made sure that I had a home to go to as well.

'It can't have been easy for them: a young married couple, lumbered with the responsibility of an eighteen-year-old student. It made the three of us very close. When they died I lost more than a brother and a sister-in-law. I lost my closest friends as well. Whatever the circumstances I would have wanted to do my best for Trixie, but when I remember the love and support Jen and Robert gave *me* . . . If I'm *over*-protective, it's because I feel I owe it to them to protect her as they would have done.'

'She's a very sensible and mature girl,' Harriet told him, unbearably moved by what he had told her. There was a large lump in her throat and her eyes stung a little with the tears she was forcing back. He had spoken so directly and so quietly, without any undue emphasis or emotionalism, and yet the stark words had reached right into her heart and touched a chord there.

'Sensible and mature she may be, but there are still situations in life which she doesn't have the experience to handle. I don't want her exposed to the kind of life the Susan Soameses of this world lead. I'm not a fool. Trixie is a very attractive young woman who'll soon want to start experimenting with life and all that that entails, but I'd much prefer it if those experiments were shared with young people of her own age and not the kind of people she's going to meet in Susan Soames's circle. She complains that I treat her like a child. I've tried to explain... I wasn't having much success, as you've probably discovered. Things have been pretty tense between us these last few weeks, culminating in that irresponsible and idiotic incident by the river.'

He paused, looked down at the ground, and then added, almost inconsequentially, 'You had every right to refuse to help me, but I was so damned angry——'

'And balked of your rightful prey,' Harriet supplied, half smiling. 'You must have been furious to discover a stranger in the car, and not Trixie.'

'Furious doesn't begin to describe it,' he agreed. 'The little wretch had deliberately pushed me into potentially the most embarrassing situation she could devise!'

'She wanted to prove a point that was important to her,' Harriet pointed out.

'Mmm. Although I'm going to miss her, I'll be glad when she's through this last year at school. Once she's at university, she'll make new friends, broaden her horizons. I know she finds it constraining living here at times. The trouble is that, with her school over twenty miles away, Eva is the only person of her age who lives locally enough for her to see on a regular basis.'

'I think you're doing Trixie an injustice if you really fear that Eva is likely to sway her own judgement.'

'Eva won't, but the whole way of life of her mother and her cronies isn't one I feel it's good for Trixie to be exposed to——'

He broke off, frowning as he saw Harriet shiver, and apologised quickly. 'I'm keeping you out in the cold. You'll be frozen. I'll see you safely inside.'

Falling into step beside him, Harriet felt a deep sense of inner happiness. For the first time they were conversing as potential friends rather than antagonists.

As she thanked him for bringing her home and unlocked the door, Harriet told herself not to place too much importance on their conversation. He was obviously worried about Trixie, and it was only natural that he should tell her as much, given the fact that he knew that Trixie liked her.

In the kitchen, she stepped out of her wet shoes and eyed them with disgust. When they dried out, she suspected they'd be unwearable. They had been expensive, but as she remembered the sensation of Rigg's hands holding her she decided recklessly that it had been worth ruining a pair of shoes to experience the pleasure of his touch.

Fool, she derided herself as she prepared for bed. She was allowing herself to nurture an impossible fantasy on the tiniest crumbs she could find.

It would be much more sensible to stop dreaming impossible dreams and concentrate instead on reality. And reality was that quite plainly Rigg felt no desire for her whatsoever.

CHAPTER SIX

IN THE morning, as soon as she had had her breakfast and driven down to the village to collect her papers, Harriet telephoned the Vicarage.

She spoke first to the Vicar's wife, and thanked her for inviting her to the party, then she asked to speak to Dan. He had gone out, Mrs Fellows informed her, and so Harriet asked her if she wouldn't mind conveying a message to him.

'We were going to have dinner tonight,' she told the other woman. 'Unfortunately I'm not going to be able to make it. I wonder if you'd give my apologies?'

When she replaced the receiver it was with a sense of relief.

She spent what was left of her Sunday morning self-indulgently reading her newspapers.

After a light lunch of home-made pasta and a couple of wholemeal rolls, she put away the papers and went outside to clean her car.

It was bitterly cold, with a sharp east wind systematically stripping off what leaves remained on the trees.

Harriet was glad of her thick jacket as she washed the car, and then put it away in the garage, locking the door behind her.

In the old days in London a whole Sunday afternoon to herself would have been a rare treat, so she couldn't understand why she should feel restless and alone.

Perhaps she ought to go ahead and get herself a dog, but if so what breed? Refusing to give in to the tempation of thinking that Rigg might be the best person to advise her, she concentrated instead on catching up with some of the household chores she had neglected during the week while she was working.

At six o'clock, when she switched on the radio, she wasn't surprised to hear that snow was forecast in the north of Scotland. The temperature had been dropping steadily all day, and she was relieved to be staying in front of a warm fire instead of having to get changed and go out on a dinner date that she hadn't wanted.

Tonight Trixie would be preparing for her return to school in the morning. Strange to think that, not so long ago, she would have been doing the same thing herself. She had enjoyed teaching, but had found the large London comprehensive over-whelming, and although she missed the contact with the eager young minds of her pupils she preferred her new way of life.

Guiltily she planned a self-indulgent evening for herself. A pizza was in the fridge for her supper, one of the dreadfully fattening ones Trixie had rec-ommended from the delicatessen in Hawick, and she intended to eat it in front of the fire while listening to the new Vivaldi tape she had bought for herself before leaving London.

When she walked through into her sitting-room an hour later, carrying her meal on a tray, she de-cided that the warm glow of the fire was sufficient light to eat by. She had already closed the curtains, and the dimly lit room felt warm and cosy.

The pizza was every bit as figure-ruining as Trixie had promised, and the glass of wine she had with it equally enjoyable. She curled up in her chair, closing her eyes as she let the magic of the music envelop her.

'Trixie, are you going to take Ben out this evening?'

Trixie removed her attention from the book she was studying, frowning slightly.

'Is it that time already?' She groaned. 'I suppose I'd better... Why on earth should any teacher want an in-depth analysis of why Trollope wrote as he did, for a half-term project? Sadists, that's what they are.'

'Hard going? Want me to take Ben for you?' Rigg offered.

She beamed at him.

'Would you? I'll make the tea for when you come back.'

At weekends they fended for themselves, leaving Mrs Arkwright free to spend her time with her family. All her children were grown up, but she had several grandchildren whose company she enjoyed. The Arkwrights owned a small cottage in the village, and it suited both her and Rigg that she didn't live in.

'Look at him, lazy dog,' Trixie commented, rubbing her bare foot over the dog's middle as he lay in front of the fire. 'Do you think he wants to go out?'

At the words the dog's ears twitched.

'Stop tormenting him,' Rigg told her, getting up. 'Come on, Ben,' he called to the dog. 'Walk!'

Immediately the Labrador was on his feet, following Rigg eagerly through the house to the back hallway, where Rigg removed a battered jacket from its peg and pulled on a pair of wellingtons.

The moment they were outside, Ben plunged ahead of Rigg, scuffling through the undergrowth, putting up a couple of indignant birds.

It was a cold, clear night, sharp with frost, with a nip in the wind that made Rigg glad of the protection of his jacket.

Ben seemed to know exactly where he wanted to go, taking the familiar path across the field and into the small belt of woodland that hid the house from the main road.

On the other side of the wood lay Harriet's cottage. Harriet... He wondered how she was enjoying her date with Dan.

There had, over the years, been several women in his life, adult, non-demanding affairs which, while physically satisfying, had been emotionally barren. He had never deliberately planned to stay single, but getting his company off the ground had taken so much of his attention and concentration, and then later there had been Trixie to consider. In eighteen months' time he would be forty. It hardly seemed possible.

He could hear Ben scuffling enthusiastically in front of him, and he called sharply to the dog, deciding it was time to return home before his thoughts became too maudlin.

When Ben didn't appear, he frowned and walked further along the path.

It crested a small rise, and below him through the trees he could see the low bulk of Harriet's cottage, and its lights.

He frowned. Its *lights*...but Harriet was out!

Calling quietly to Ben, he set off in the direction of the cottage, his frown deepening. It seemed unlikely that anyone *should* have broken in, but crime and violence were so unpredictable these days that such assumptions were not necessarily the correct ones.

Even out here, in this quiet, remote part of the country, they had their share of robberies. There had been a spate of them recently, a gang from Newcastle, the police suspected, systematically going through the small villages.

Several people had heard Dan making his date with Harriet. She was newly arrived from London and, while not precisely wealthy, not poor either.

All these, and several other thoughts as well, ran through his brain as he approached the cottage, Ben obeying his silent command to come to heel.

Rigg had trained the dog as a pup, and although Trixie was inclined to spoil him, the Labrador knew quite well when it was important to respond to his master's command.

As Rigg circled the front of the house, he saw that it was in darkness and that it was the kitchen that was brilliantly illuminated.

When he looked through the window there was no evidence of any interlopers.

He tried the door handle automatically, and frowned when it turned under his hand, revealing that the door was unlocked. Still frowning he opened the door and walked in.

* * *

It was the silence that woke Harriet from her lazy doze, to realise that the tape had finished. Sleepily she stretched and started to get up, freezing when she heard the unmistakable sounds of someone moving around in the kitchen.

Her blood chilled with the horrible recognition of the fact that she had left the back door unlocked—something she would never have dreamed of doing in London. Her telephone was in the kitchen.

She glanced wildly towards the front of the house, wondering if she would have time to escape through the locked front door before the intruder could reach her, and then acknowledging that she wouldn't. The front door was bolted and locked and the key was hanging up in the kitchen. Too late now to long for that dog she had been wondering about getting, the larger and fiercer the better.

She heard footsteps coming towards the sitting-room door, and glanced wildly round, looking for something with which to defend herself.

The only thing she could see was the poker. She picked it up, holding it nervously, her mouth dry with tension as the door opened inwards, and a tall, male, and surely familiar figure walked in.

Rigg! She let the poker drop from her hands, as relief made her tremble violently.

'Rigg!'

'Harriet!'

The both spoke at the same time, and then both stopped.

'What are you——?'

'I thought you were out——'

Once again they both stopped.

Then Rigg said curtly, 'I'm sorry about this. I must have scared you half to death, but I saw the lights on when I was walking Ben, and believing you were out——'

'It's all right,' Harriet told him shakily. 'I'm grateful you were concerned enough to check. I cancelled my date with Dan.' She turned her back to him and said in a low voice. 'He rather anticipated my acceptance, and I didn't want to embarrass him by refusing him in public.'

She was starting to gabble nervously, not so much because of the release of fear, but because of Rigg—because he was here, standing only inches away from her, in the firelight, in the intimacy of her sitting-room.

She shuddered suddenly.

'Look, I've given you a bad shock. Sit down for a few minutes, and I'll make you a drink.'

'No, no, it's all right,' Harriet fibbed. 'Thank goodness I realised it was you.' She glanced ruefully at where the poker lay on the floor, and then suddenly the realisation of how easily she might actually have injured him with it overwhelmed her and she started to tremble violently, burying her face in her hands as she fought to control the wave of emotion that rocked her.

The sensation of Rigg reaching out towards her and taking hold of her, wrapping her in his arms, his chin resting on the top of her head as he soothed her, rocking her gently in his arms, stunned her.

Shudder after shudder tore through her as Harriet tried to blot out the tormenting image of Rigg lying at her feet, blood oozing from the head wound she herself had inflicted. Thank God she had recognised him in time.

As though he read her mind, he said quietly against her forehead, 'Stop thinking about it. It didn't happen.'

His voice sent tiny reverberations of sensation zigzagging over her skin. So acute was her awareness of him that the tiny hairs in the nape of her neck lifted and her body tensed as she instinctively fought against the sensual heat his touch was releasing inside her.

'I'm sorry about this,' she told him unsteadily, lifting her head from his shoulder and trying to pull back from him.

His jacket had been cold to her touch, and somehow or other she had moved her hands beneath it so that they were resting against the soft wool of his shirt. She could feel the warm live maleness of him beneath her fingertips, his body hard and warm, tautly muscled, different from her own. She wanted to reach out and allow herself the indulgence of exploring the hard muscles beneath his shirt, to trace the breadth of his collarbone and to place her lips against the hollow at the base of his throat.

He had brought into the room with him a disturbing masculine atmosphere against which she had no protection. He smelled of clean, cold fresh air, woodsmoke and, disturbingly, something else, musky and very male. She wanted to bury her face in his throat and breathe in that magical scent, to savour his taste with her tongue and her lips.

The strength of her own desire stunned her, holding her immobile as she stared up at him, her eyes dark with shock and confusion. She tried to step back from him automatically, terrified that he would sense what she was feeling and be as appalled as she was herself, but he wasn't letting her go. His hands slid down her back to her waist and rested lightly there.

Was she imagining that they had slid down over her back with slow sensuality? she wondered dizzily, her hands clutching at his arms for support as she tried desperately to force herself back to reality. It was one thing to know how much she loved and desired him, but it was another thing entirely to start imagining that *he* might desire *her*.

She fixed her gaze on the shadowy darkness beyond his shoulder, and took one deep steadying breath and then another.

'Harriet.'

He said her name softly, and she responded automatically to his voice, turning her head to look at him.

It was a mistake.

Her eyes were almost on the same level as his mouth. She trembled as she watched it frame her name for a second time, her own lips suddenly parting.

This was madness. She must be going crazy, imagining... She lifted her head and looked into his eyes, trying to control her rioting emotions, and then her heart turned over inside her as she saw the way he was watching her, and knew, quite without doubt, that he was going to kiss her.

She could have stopped him... *could* have avoided the slow descent of his head, the gentle pressure of the hands that brought her up against his body. She *could* have done so, but why should she, when she had been dreaming of a moment like this almost from the first time she had seen him?

She felt herself tremble as his mouth brushed hers, a sudden rush of dizzying emotion engulfing her.

Without knowing it, she made a small anguished sound in her throat, and for a moment Rigg hesitated, his mouth stilling against her own, but then, when she made no move to step back from him, his hands slid from her waist up over her back until they cupped her face, holding it, tilting it, so that she was eagerly helpless beneath the pressure of his kiss.

She had been kissed before, but never had she imagined that it was possible for a mere kiss to unleash such sensations as she felt now. When Rigg's fingers slid into her hair, she clung eagerly to him, winding her arms around him, returning the demanding pressure of his mouth without any thought of concealing from him what he was doing to her.

She could feel the aching tension gripping her body, the ache in her breasts as she pressed as close to him as she could.

His mouth left hers, his hand pushing her hair out of the way so that he could taste the soft skin of her throat. She trembled as she felt his lips caressing the delicate cord that pulsed beneath her skin. His teeth tormented her sensitive flesh, making her cry out and press her own hot mouth into the hollow of flesh exposed by the open neck of his shirt.

It was only when he jerked back from her as though her touch stung that she came to her senses and realised what she was doing.

Immediately she pulled out of his arms, and turned her back on him so that he couldn't see the burning betrayal of her skin.

She sensed him behind her, moving towards her, and her whole body tensed. Please, God, don't let him say anything, she prayed. Please, please just make him go...

It seemed her prayer was answered. He stopped and then said curtly, 'I'd better go. Don't forget to lock the door after me, will you?'

Harriet didn't turn round until she was quite sure he had gone, half running into the kitchen to do as he had instructed. Once the door was locked, she leaned against it, pressing her hot face to the cold wood, shaking as though she had a fever.

What on earth had possessed her? What on *earth* must he be thinking? There could have been no mistaking her over-passionate response to what he had probably intended to be merely a casual embrace. Humiliation scalded her. She had probably embarrassed *him* almost as much as she had embarrassed herself. He hadn't been able to wait to get away... Responding to him like that, like a— like a sex-starved... Oh, God... She buried her face in her hands, giving way to the emotions which racked her.

On Sunday night Harriet barely slept. She woke up on Monday morning with a nagging ache of tension in her temples.

When she looked at herself in the mirror as she washed, the wan reflection staring back at her made her grimace in disgust.

Over and over again through her mind rolled a continuous film of those minutes in Rigg's arms. Over and over again, reinforcing what she already knew: that her reaction to what on his part had probably only been a momentary impulse, an automatic male reaction to the fact that she was in his arms, had been way over the top.

No wonder he had hurried off like that, his set face registering shock. She had embarrassed him and made a fool of herself.

Embarrassed him? A man who had managed to endure with complete *savoir-faire* the trick which Trixie had played on him?

All day long, even though she knew the last thing he was likely to do was to arrive on her doorstep, she was tensely dreading the ring of the telephone or, even worse, a knock on the door.

So much so that by late afternoon she had a pounding sick headache and her stomach muscles were cramped and taut.

She had no idea how on earth she was ever going to face him again. The best she could hope for was that he would politely ignore what had happened.

Every time she allowed herself to remember what had happened her face went hot with humiliation. She tried to tell herself that it was pointless to dwell on something that was now best forgotten. She also tried to tell herself that Rigg might misconstrue the reason for the intensity of her response, and put it down to the fact that she had had a bad fright.

And pigs might fly, she added mentally and derisively. In that shocked, dazed look he had given her in those few illuminating seconds before he turned away from her, she had seen the truth.

She was glad that Trixie was back at school and unlikely to come calling on her, even though she missed the younger girl's chatter, and then, when late in the afternoon she finally acknowledged that whatever work she had managed to get through that day was all too likely to end up in the waste-paper bin, she remembered that she had promised to have dinner with Trixie and Rigg on Saturday.

As she stared unseeingly into space, she wondered desperately how on earth she could possibly face Rigg. She searched desperately through her brain for an acceptable excuse for refusing to go with them.

A vital visit to her publishers, perhaps? But that would mean that she'd have to spend the weekend in London, and then there was Trixie. Rigg had told her specifically that Trixie wanted her to be there.

After all, she was going to have to face him sooner or later. Perhaps if she concentrated very hard, and acted as though nothing untoward had happened, she might be able to persuade him that nothing had...

A deep frown furrowed her forehead. Perhaps if she acted completely naturally, Rigg might think that she always responded like that when men kissed her.

Whatever he thought, he would certainly be relieved that she wasn't reading something into his kiss that hadn't been there.

All evening she tussled with the problem of what she ought to do, balancing her own cowardly desire to bury her head in the sand and never ever have to face him again, and the strong streak of loyalty and responsibility that was so much a part of her nature, and which told her that it was unfair to Trixie to refuse to attend her birthday celebration.

As she prepared for bed, she remembered that she had intended to ask Rigg's advice about getting a dog. Impossible to do that now. She shuddered deeply, imagining all too well the motivation he would think lay behind her appeal for his advice.

Foolish she might be—foolish indeed to have fallen in love so deeply and carelessly at her age—but she had her pride, and sensitively she cringed from the thought of his suspecting quite wrongly that she was trying to pursue him.

For a second night in succession she slept badly, waking up feeling unrefreshed and tense.

It was a cold frosty morning, and despite the central heating the cold seemed to have penetrated her bones. When she drank her breakfast mug of coffee she wrapped her hands tightly around the mug as though she could draw its warmth into her chilled body.

An absent-minded glance into the mirror when she walked into the bathroom showed her that what she was feeling was betrayed by her pale, drawn face.

She was being ridiculous, she told herself sternly. Love-sickness was something that could be tolerated in a teenager, but not in a woman of her age. It was time she pulled herself together, gave her thoughts a new direction. So she had made a fool of herself; it was pointless torturing herself by going over and over what had happened. It had happened, and now the best thing she could do was to convince Rigg that, despite her passionately intense reaction to him, the incident was to be forgotten.

Outside the sun was shining on a perfect autumn day. She had things to do, a birthday present to get for Trixie, letters to post. If she was going to redecorate her sitting-room, then she would need paint and paper. Her work was progressing nicely, or at least it had been until yesterday. She could afford to take some time off.

Remembering that a local free newspaper had been delivered with her letters on Saturday morning, she riffled through the contents of the wire basket she used as an in-tray and fished it out.

Hadn't she intended, when she moved up here, to do some ferreting about, and buy herself some sturdy, comfortable country furniture?

The local news-sheet carried the information that there was a cattle market today in one of the nearby small towns. She had never seen a cattle market in progress. It would be interesting to do so.

Determinedly she changed her clothes, and, having checked that the house was securely locked, climbed into her car. The small town that was her destination lay nestling against its surrounding hills, basking in the bright sunshine that turned the stone houses a rich warm gold. The town was busy, and Harriet was thankful that her small car was easy to park.

As she walked past a bookshop a book in the window on the town's history caught her eye and she went in and bought it. She hadn't realised that the town had once been the site of a large and very wealthy priory.

As she glanced through the book over a cup of coffee in a small, pretty café tucked away down a cobbled side-street, she read that the majority of the older houses in the town had been built from stone taken from the site of the ruined priory after its destruction had been ordered by Henry VIII. Like so many of the Border towns, this one had a violent and bloody past. Mary, Queen of Scots, had stayed here overnight, so legend went.

The smiling waitress who had taken Harriet's order was only too pleased to give her directions to the cattle market.

'Local cheese and eggs they sell there, as well as fresh vegetables,' she advised Harriet, 'and much cheaper than in the supermarkets.'

Thanking her, Harriet put on her coat and went back outside.

A small art gallery several doors away from the café caught her eye next, and she paused outside it, staring at the portrait in the window, her heart leaping chokingly into her throat.

The man in it, soberly garbed in black, his profile stern and hard, might have been Rigg, despite his sixteenth-century clothes.

Angry with herself, she forced herself to walk away. This was ridiculous. She had come here to get away from her obsessive thoughts about Rigg.

She found the cattle market quite easily, and wandered around the stalls of produce set up close by, buying some of the cheese and the eggs recommended by the girl in the café, as well as some locally grown vegetables.

The soft accent of the Borders washed all round her, and the quiet purposefulness of the locals' movements was soothing and relaxing after the impatient bustle of London's streets. Whatever it might cost her in emotional heartache to have come here, there was no denying that the countryside and its people had a special magic. At the stalls where she bought things, the stallholders had a warm smile for her, and time to exchange a few pleasantries.

She paused close to the market, watching an older man enjoying the sunshine outside the ancient pub that dominated the small square. As she looked upwards and saw its battered swinging sign, Harriet smiled gently.

The Drover's Arms. Of course, this town like so many others would have lain along the route the drovers took, when they came down from the hills with their flocks.

She paused to look into a local estate agent's window, and read a notice of forthcoming auctions. One for the contents of several farms and houses caught her eye and she made a note of its date.

What she hankered for was an old-fashioned dresser, and if possible an old-fashioned farmhouse-style dinner service to go with it. Such things fetched fantastic prices in London, where every basement kitchen was being fitted with country-style kitchen units and the all-important, newly fashionable Aga. Perhaps up here things might not be quite as expensive.

The town had a small park laid out in what had once been the grounds of the priory, and Harriet spent some time there feeding the wildfowl on the

river which ran through it, before reminding herself
that she had not yet found a present for Trixie.

This part of the world was famous for its wools
and tweeds, and while she suspected that Trixie was
hardly likely to welcome anything in tweed, despite
the fact that it had shed its old-fashioned, heavy,
scratchy image, she remembered that the town
boasted a woollen mill with its own shop.

She found it on the outskirts of the town, a reno-
vated building with a now picturesque waterwheel.
The small shop was well laid out and the girl
working there helpful.

Harriet explained what she wanted, and the girl
smiled at her.

'I think we've got something that might appeal.
I've been drooling over them myself.'

She was in her early twenties, clear skinned, with
soft brown hair and sherry-coloured eyes that
danced when she smiled.

'They're the work of a local designer,' she told
Harriet, turning away from her to open a drawer
in the cupboards behind her.

'A sort of Kaffe Fassett design. We don't stock
many, because they're all individually made and
rather pricy.'

She turned back to the counter, gently unfolding
a sweater which made Harriet catch her breath with
pleasure at the wonderful mingling of autumn
colours in a design that constantly drew the eye
without tiring it.

'Feel it,' the girl offered. 'It's local wool. Beautifully soft.'

It was, Harriet recognised.

'There's a matching hat and scarf.'

Already she could see Trixie wearing the trio of sweater, scarf and hat. They might have been especially designed for her with her colouring.

'How much?' Harriet enquired, knowing that no matter how much she searched she would never find anything as ideal.

The girl was right; they were expensive, but not overpriced for the workmanship and style.

Ten minutes later, with her purchases wrapped up, Harriet headed back for the main shopping street to buy wrapping paper and a card.

An eighteenth birthday was something of a very special event; she had been a little surprised that Trixie hadn't opted for a party with her friends, but Rigg had told her that Trixie had elected to wait until she was twenty-one for such an affair.

Buoyed up by the pleasure of having found a present that she was sure Trixie would love, she set off back to her car, acknowledging that her decision to come out had been the right one. Already she felt more relaxed, more optimistic about her ability to force herself to get over her ridiculous feelings for Rigg.

Then, as she turned a corner, she stopped dead, the blood draining from her face, her heartbeat accelerating dangerously, as she saw Rigg walking along the street, not five yards away from her, deep in conversation with another man.

The urge to turn round and run the other way before he saw her was overpowering. Her mouth went dry. Another moment and he would lift his head and see her.

She held her breath, desperate to escape before he did and yet at the same time rooted to the spot where she stood, and then, without even looking in her direction, he and his companion turned into a narrow side-street and disappeared from her view.

Blinking slowly, she stared around the now empty street. Had she actually seen him, or had she simply imagined it? Her heart was thumping frantically. She felt sick and faintly dizzy.

Somehow or other she managed to make her way back to her car, but once there she had to sit behind the wheel for several minutes before she felt able to set the car in motion and drive back home.

Why couldn't she control her emotions? Why couldn't she banish this unwanted and dangerous love from her life? Why couldn't she behave like the mature woman she was? Outwardly she was a woman of thirty-four, but inwardly she was as vulnerable as a girl of eighteen. More so, perhaps... It couldn't go on. She must find some way of getting her emotions under control. But how?

CHAPTER SEVEN

ALL week, Harriet deliberately kept herself very busy, hoping in that way to block out the too intrusive memories of her intensely passionate response to Rigg's kiss, and the self-contempt and anguish which had followed it.

It didn't work, of course. Every night when she eventually went to bed, physically exhausted by the frenetically filled hours of the day, she still lay sleepless and on edge, fighting against her body's treacherous desire not only to relive that kiss, but also to allow her imagination full rein to carry her past the kiss and on to deeper intimacies.

This urge stunned her; she had never considered herself to be a deeply passionate woman. Those men whom she had dated had never touched the deep wellspring of sensation that Rigg seemed to have found so unerringly.

Simply by closing her eyes and allowing herself to drift away from reality, she could swiftly conjure up not only how she had felt in Rigg's arms, but how she *would* have felt if he had not released her, but . . .

Sweat broke out on her skin as she tried to control her wayward thoughts—thoughts surely more suitable for a young girl on the verge of a sexual awakening than an adult woman. Only, as a young girl, *she* had never imagined it was possible to feel like this, to want like this, to ache like this so that the sensation inside her almost physically hurt.

The only good thing to come out of the whole miserable episode was the fact that she had actually started work on the new book, Harriet acknowledged grimly on Thursday afternoon.

Normally slow and cautious in relation to her writing, she had been surprised by the speed with which what had been no more than a vague idea had taken shape, not only in her mind, but on actual pages of typescript. And the more she wrote the more the scope of the finished novel grew both in breadth and in length. What had started as no more than a vague idea was developing so quickly that at times Harriet herself felt half overwhelmed by it.

If she continued with it, she was going to have to do a great deal of research, and she had still not even approached her publishers to discuss what she was doing with them.

That they might not be interested in accepting a very long novel from her that was aimed not at the children's market but at the adult, was something she was well aware of, and yet despite that the book was insisting on being written.

Now, rereading the work she had done that week, she was immediately struck by the main male character's similarity to Rigg. Guiltily she gnawed at her bottom lip. In using some of Rigg's characteristics for her hero, even if she had done so unconsciously, she felt as though she were intruding into private and guarded areas of his life without an invitation.

Telling herself that she was being oversensitive, and that even with the remote possibility of the book ever being published it was hardly likely that Rigg would read it, she concentrated on the typescript in front of her.

The phone rang, just as she was becoming involved in the unfolding of the story. At first she tried to ignore its imperious summons, but then, when she realised that whoever was ringing wasn't going to ring off, she got up to answer it.

The sound of Rigg's voice almost made her drop the receiver, an electric current of painful pleasure ripping through her body as she gripped the receiver tightly, unable to speak.

'Harriet, are you there? Harriet?'

Her mouth had gone dry, her heart was pounding. She felt light-headed as though she had a fever.

'Yes. I'm here, Rigg.'

How on earth had she managed to make her voice sound so normal, so calm and controlled, when in reality...when in reality she was trembling inwardly beneath the surge of complex emotions that hearing his voice evoked?

'I'm just ringing to sort out the arrangements for Saturday evening. It seems pointless travelling in separate cars when you're so close, so if we picked you up about seven-thirty...'

Harriet hesitated, knowing that the less time she spent in Rigg's company the easier the evening would be to bear, and yet knowing also that she couldn't very well insist on travelling alone, not when she was their guest.

'I... Thank you. I'll be ready,' she told him.

She wondered what he was thinking, if he was dreading Saturday as much as she was herself.

The speed with which he had withdrawn from her on Sunday evening had made it plain how little he had welcomed her passionate response to him.

Had he recognised what lay behind it, or did he simply think that she had been momentarily physically carried away? She hoped it was the latter. She didn't know how she was going to endure it if he had guessed that she had fallen in love with him.

Fallen in love. How ridiculously juvenile it sounded, but there was nothing juvenile about the way she was feeling, far from it.

'I've booked a table for us at a hotel just outside Hawick,' he was saying to her. 'Their dinner dances have a very good reputation.'

Harriet mumbled something in response.

'We'll see you on Saturday then, at seven-thirty,' finished Rigg.

'Yes... Yes. Saturday at seven-thirty,' Harriet agreed.

Long after she had replaced the receiver, she was still staring blankly into space, her stomach churning.

A dinner dance. She had thought they were simply going out for dinner. She longed to be able to pick up the phone and ring Trixie and tell her that she just could not join them, but of course it was impossible.

Trixie's actual birthday was on the Friday, and, feeling safe in the knowledge that Rigg would be at the factory outside Hawick that produced the computer parts he designed and sold, she drove round to the house late in the afternoon.

Trixie had just returned from school and welcomed Harriet enthusiastically, showing her the cards and gifts she had received from her schoolfriends. 'Eva's having an all-night disco to celebrate her eighteenth,' she told Harriet as Harriet handed over her own gift. Trixie was making a face. 'Small chance of Rigg allowing me to have anything like that. I wish he'd let me go skiing with them. I used to go with Mum and Dad, you know. They both loved it. Rigg's taken me on holiday a couple of times, but never skiing.'

For a moment she looked very downcast, but then she brightened up, her gloom forgotten as she saw what Harriet had bought her.

'Oh, Harriet, it's wonderful,' she enthused, smoothing the soft wool and then holding it up in front of her.

'Look at this, Mrs Arkwright,' she demanded of the housekeeper. 'Isn't it absolutely ace?'

As she danced round the kitchen, holding the sweater in front of her, she told Harriet gleefully, 'I've been wanting one for simply ages, but they cost the earth. Just wait until Eva sees it! Oh, Harriet, you're wonderful,' she announced, putting the sweater down and coming over and giving Harriet a quick hug.

To her own astonishment, Harriet felt her eyes sting with tears as she returned Trixie's hug.

In her own family physical demonstrations of affection had been rare. Her father had been a remote, almost withdrawn man, her mother fussy and sometimes impatient. Even Louise, who had regularly coaxed out of her sums of money she could not really afford for things for the twins and herself, had never repaid her generosity with anything more than a casual 'Thanks.'

'I can't wait to wear it,' Trixie was crowing, returning to stroke the soft wool with admiring fingers.

'To wear what?'

The sound of Rigg's voice made Harriet retreat instinctively further into the shadows by the door.

She hadn't heard him arrive, and as he walked into the kitchen her senses clung greedily to the reality of him. He had brought in with him the scent of cold clean air. His dark hair was tousled by the strong wind, and his movements were lithe and well co-ordinated as he shrugged off his jacket and repeated, 'To wear what?'

'This,' Trixie told him, picking up Harriet's gift. 'Harriet's given it to me.'

'Harriet.'

Was she imagining the sharp note of dislike in his voice as he swung round, searching the room?

She couldn't bring herself to meet his eyes.

'I'm glad you like it,' she told Trixie huskily. 'I must go.'

'Oh, no, not yet,' Trixie protested. 'Mrs Arkwright has baked me a cake. Stay and have a piece with us. Make her stay, Rigg.'

Make her stay... Harriet was pretty sure that that was the last thing he would want to do. He must be as anxious for her to be gone as she was herself.

She was quite sure that she was not imagining that quick frown that touched his forehead, as he said sharply, 'I don't have any jurisdiction over Harriet, Trixie. If she has other things to do——'

'Oh, you don't, do you?' Trixie asked her quickly. 'After all it *is* my birthday!'

Even though she knew that that wistfulness was probably contrived, Harriet found it impossible to resist.

'Well, I——'

'Good, you're staying.'

Harriet couldn't help looking in Rigg's direction, but he had his back to her and was saying something quietly to Mrs Arkwright.

As he turned back to them, he said easily, 'Come on, then. Mrs Arkwright is going to bring the cake into the drawing-room.'

'The drawing-room?' Trixie's eyebrows rose. 'But we always have tea in your study.'

'Not today,' Rigg told her firmly, crossing the kitchen and opening the door for them.

The drawing-room occupied almost the full depth of the house. It had long graceful windows that looked out across the gardens. A warm log fire burned in the huge grate, giving off a welcome warmth, but Harriet noticed that the room was also heated by some discreetly placed radiators.

'This room was already furnished when I bought the house.'

The sound of Rigg's voice so close to her ear made Harriet tense. Didn't he remember how vulnerable she was to him? Couldn't he see the effect he was having on her simply by standing here so close to her? Too close to her, she acknowledged as her body reacted to his proximity, her stomach muscles tensing against the aching, yielding sensation melting through her lower body in an unstoppable tide of slow heat.

'It's very nice,' she responded jerkily, cursing herself for the inanity of her comment.

Obviously he was trying to do his best to ignore what had happened on Sunday, either out of good manners or maybe even as a subtle means of warning her off reading too much into it. And if she had any sense at all she would respond to his easy sophistication with matching casualness.

But when did a person in love ever behave with good sense?

She was torn between taking to her heels and putting as much distance between them as she could, and closing that small distance between them so that her body touched his.

'Nice?' Trixie, who had overheard her comment, wrinkled her nose. 'I suppose it is if you like all this old stuff...'

A wave of her arm indicated the comfortably worn damask-covered chairs and sofa, the damask slightly worn in places and faded in a way that Harriet personally felt lent great charm to a room which without that softening homely touch could have appeared overpoweringly grand.

It was a large room, the major part of a wing that had been added to the original house at a later date, and the plasterwork on its ceiling and cornices suggested that whoever had designed it had been an admirer of the work of Robert Adam.

A well-worn carpet mirrored the plasterwork design on the ceiling.

'I wanted Rigg to throw out the whole lot,' Trixie told her, grimacing. 'But he wouldn't.'

'I like it,' Harriet said softly. 'It ... it feels right.'

She coloured up when she saw the way Trixie was looking at her, and then to her surprise heard Rigg's voice.

'That's exactly what I thought. The house had been in the same family for generatons before I bought it. This room had first been furnished by the previous owner's mother-in-law. It would have been easy enough to get designers in to refurbish it, but I felt that the furnishings in here went with the house, somehow.'

It was plain that Trixie was about to argue with him, but before she could speak Mrs Arkwright came in, pushing an old-fashioned wooden trolley.

On it was not only a beautifully iced birthday cake, but also plates of tiny thin sandwiches, a large pot of tea, and several plates of assorted small cakes and scones.

Trixie saw Harriet's face and grinned.

'It's Rigg's fault,' she told her. 'He has a thing about "afternoon tea"——'

'A self-indulgence I can heartily recommend,' Rigg interrupted smoothly.

He thanked Mrs Arkwright and then, as she left the room, asked Harriet, 'Would you do the honours, Harriet?'

Once upon a time, it had been a test of a young girl's social ability to be asked to perform such a task.

The teapot was silver and heavy, but it poured perfectly. Watching the stream of golden liquid filling the cups and recognising its scent, Harriet asked automatically, 'Earl Grey?'

'What else?' Rigg replied smiling.

But Trixie said teasingly, 'Personally I prefer tea-bags.'

She had brought her cards and presents into the drawing-room and was busy showing them to Rigg.

By rights she ought to have felt uncomfortable and out of place here, Harriet reflected, watching them as she sipped her hot, delicious tea, and yet oddly she didn't. Now that the shock of Rigg's arrival had worn off, and now that her heartbeat had returned to something approaching normal, she was aware of a feeling of great contentment and happiness—a sense of coming home and of being with people whose company would never pall.

Despite her teasing of Rigg, it was Trixie who made the largest inroads into the sandwiches and scones. She was a slender girl with boundless energy, and Harriet was glad to see her eating well. Louise had always been a faddy eater, complaining that she had to watch her figure, making Harriet feel both greedy and guilty when she refused to share her sparse meals.

'Well, I think it's time I cut the cake,' Trixie announced, standing up, but Rigg checked her, and then walked to the door and disappeared through it.

While Trixie was still frowning her lack of comprehension he was back, and Mrs Arkwright and her husband with him. He was also carrying a bottle of champagne, and Mrs Arkwright had a tray in her hands on which were five chilled champagne glasses.

Harriet saw the way Trixie's face suddenly glowed with colour and pleasure, as Rigg ceremoniously opened the champagne and then poured them all a glass.

'To you, Trixie,' he said softly, toasting her, and as they all raised their glasses to her, Harriet knew indubitably that Rigg was thinking about his brother and sister-in-law whose child Trixie was and who had not lived to see their daughter grow to maturity.

For a moment sadness seemed to permeate the air of the room, so that Harriet felt a lump come up into her throat and instinctively her head turned towards Rigg, their glances meeting. She could see the sadness in his eyes, and her own self-contempt and embarrassment were forgotten as she watched him in silent sympathy.

'The cake...I must cut the cake,' Trixie was saying, her voice banishing the sadness from Rigg's eyes as he teased her.

'Do you mean to say you've still got room for cake after all those sandwiches?'

And then both Mrs Arkwright and her husband were hugging Trixie and congratulating her, giving her a small gift which she unwrapped with unspoilt pleasure and enthusiasm.

She was such a warm, loving girl, Harriet reflected, watching the small tableau. She warmed everyone she came in contact with; a rare gift which Rigg obviously recognised and cherished.

He waited until the champagne and cake were disposed of before reaching into his suit pocket and giving Trixie his own gift, a flat, oblong package which looked very much to Harriet as though it contained jewellery.

Trixie took it uncertainly.

'But you've already given me my present,' she told him uncertainly. 'You said my car was to be my eighteenth birthday present.'

'Which it was,' Rigg agreed calmly. Then, directing her attention to the gift tag attached to the present, he added quietly, 'But this isn't really from me.'

Trixie read the card in silence, and Harriet saw her mouth tremble slightly as she unwrapped it with unsteady fingers.

When she opened it she gave a small gasp, and then turning to Harriet said shakily, 'Oh, Harriet, look . . . my mother's pearls . . .'

There were tears in her eyes, and Harriet found that she herself felt equally emotional.

How thoughtful of Rigg to have given her such a gift.

'I've had them cleaned and restrung,' Rigg was saying calmly, but Trixie whirled round while he was still speaking and flung herself into his arms.

'Oh, Rigg, I do love you,' she said huskily.

Watching while he held Trixie, rocking her comfortingly, Harriet knew that from now on there would never be a second of her life in which this man did not fill her heart and mind.

As he released Trixie, Harriet stepped back from them, instinctively turning her back on them, frightened that Rigg might look at her and see what she was thinking.

While Trixie's happy chatter filled the room, she tried to come to terms with what she was feeling.

To have fallen in love with Rigg was bad enough, but at least then she had tried to tell herself that her feelings, if painful, were like a dose of a particularly virulent and unpleasant flu, acutely distressing at the time, but quickly over. Now she knew she had been wrong. There was nothing impermanent or fleeting about the way she felt.

She would love Rigg until the end of her life.

She shivered so unexpectedly and so violently that the glass in her hand trembled.

'Harriet's cold,' Trixie said innocently, seeing her shudder.

Her face pale with anguish and despair, Harriet saw the quick frown that touched Rigg's forehead.

'No, I'm fine,' she lied valiantly, 'but I really must go. I only called round to bring Trixie's present.'

'Oh, no, please stay——' Trixie started to plead, but Rigg cut her off with a cold warning word.

'Trixie.'

When she stopped and looked at him, he added coolly, 'Harriet has a life of her own, you know. I'm sure she has far more important things to do than spend the evening with us.'

Harriet almost denied it, but good sense stopped her, and although Trixie gave her a thoughtful look she didn't continue to press her to stay.

Good manners dictated that Rigg walked with her to her car, and Harriet was relieved that Trixie elected to join him.

She still felt far too vulnerable, too cringingly aware of her earlier behaviour to feel anything other than on edge and uncomfortable alone with him.

He opened the car door for her, his arm brushing hers as she got into the driver's seat. Immediately she tensed, her body tinglingly aware of him. His dark head bent towards her as he wished her goodbye, and immediately she remembered how she had felt watching the descent of his mouth towards her own on Sunday.

She was still trembling as she drove away, wishing there was some way she could avoid having dinner with them tomorrow.

She slept as she had done all week, in short bursts, burdened with fraught nerve-racking dreams that involved Rigg, and from which her subconscious firmly dragged her. When morning eventually came she felt tired and drained, her eyes gritty from lack of proper sleep, her brain dulled by the continual effort of keeping at bay the hopeless dreams which tormented her.

Halfway through Saturday morning, she suddenly recognised that if she was going to a dinner dance she would need something to wear. She so rarely went out that there was nothing in her wardrobe remotely suitable for such an occasion.

Biting her lip, she told herself sternly that it was vanity and nothing else that insisted she needed something new to wear. There was that eminently sensible black velvet skirt she had had for several years.

Eminently sensible and eminently dull, an inner voice taunted her.

If Rigg hadn't been one of the party, would she be going to such trouble? she demanded of herself half an hour later as she drove towards Hawick. Her hands tightened on the wheel as she acknowledged the mental jibe.

But she still didn't turn back, and once in Hawick she didn't waste any time, but headed straight for the same small shop where she had bought her red suit.

The same girl came forward to help her, recognising her and welcoming her with a warm smile.

Uncertainly Harriet explained what she was after, telling the girl where she was going.

'I don't want anything too over the top,' she added as a sop to her own uncomfortable conscience. 'I'm not quite sure what sort of thing will be appropriate.'

'Well, at this time of the year people do tend to dress up more,' the girl told her with a smile. 'And that particular hotel does have a clientèle that sets very high standards.'

She saw Harriet's expression and smiled sympathetically.

'I know what you mean, though, don't worry. Obviously you don't want a dress so individual that you can't wear it again. My Christmas stock has just arrived, so I've got several things I can show you.'

In the end Harriet opted for a dress in rich blue silk velvet that clung to her body from her shoulders down to her hips before flaring out into a rustling taffeta skirt over a net petticoat.

She had suggested initially that the dress was both too short and too young for her, but the girl had laughed, so genuinely amused by her comment that Harriet had allowed herself to be convinced that she was wrong.

Even so, despite its high round neck and long sleeves, there was something about the fit of the silk velvet body of the dress that made it surprisingly provocative. Too provocative for someone like her? Harriet wondered uneasily, but it was already too late. The girl was wrapping the dress carefully in tissue and packing it away in a carrier bag.

'If you need shoes, there's a shop several doors down that have a good selection,' she advised Harriet.

Sighing a little over her own uncharacteristic extravagance, Harriet had to acknowledge that she would need shoes. The only pair she had which were remotely suitable for evening wear were black.

As the girl in the dress shop had suggested, she found an excellent variety in the shoe shop several doors away and eventually left, having bought not only a pair of high-heeled dark blue satin evening shoes, but additionally a matching evening bag.

All this just for one occasion, but then she could not have gone wearing her old black velvet skirt.

Why not? she asked herself drily as she drove back home. After all, she had worn it for the last seven successive Christmases without thinking it needed replacing.

But a dinner dance was rather different from the school parties for which she had originally bought her black velvet, she reminded herself.

It didn't matter how much she tried to rationalise her purchases to herself, in her heart of hearts she knew she had bought them with one person in mind. Rigg.

Harriet was rapidly discovering that those emotions and impulses which she had naïvely thought belonged only to the teenage years were not something that conveniently went away as one got older, and that she was just as capable of falling in love and losing her head as a girl of Trixie's age.

Perhaps even more capable, she acknowledged mentally.

Despite the fact that she had allowed herself plenty of time, at twenty past seven she was still not ready. She had washed and blow-dried her hair, and put on her make-up and her dress, but then, on studying her reflection in the mirror, decided that she looked more as though she were trying to imitate a girl of twenty than appear a woman in her mid-thirties.

Firmly she swept up her hair, determined to secure it in the neat knot she had always worn for school, but her fingers, once so skilled at performing this task, suddenly refused to co-operate with her. The result was that when she heard Rigg's car outside she was still battling with her hair.

Tense with nerves, uncomfortably aware of the extra special care she had taken with her appearance, dreading that Rigg would take one look at her, and see through all her carefully erected defences to the vulnerability of what was in her heart, she was forced to concede defeat. So she allowed her hair to tumble down on to her shoulders, and was able to give it only a cursory run-through with her brush before she grabbed her evening bag and hurried downstairs.

As she locked the door she heard Rigg ring the front bell. Since she didn't have an evening coat as such, she snatched up a soft mohair jacket she had originally knitted for Louise, who had complained once it was finished that cream wasn't her colour.

Since the wool had been prohibitively expensive, and since Louise had nagged her into buying it in the first place, Harriet had been reluctant to throw the jacket to one side and it had ended up in her own wardrobe, never worn until now.

Unaware of how well the soft wool became her own colouring, enhancing the tone of her skin, and adding to her soft air of femininity, she hugged the jacket protectively around her as she opened the door and acknowledged Rigg's greeting with a tight smile.

As soon as she had locked the door she hurried out to the Range Rover, terrified that he would feel that good manners obliged him to make some comment on her appearance. She felt as though her dress had the words 'brand new' written all over it, and that he must immediately guess why she had gone to such trouble.

Instinctively she went to the rear door of the Range Rover, only to discover that Trixie and a young man Harriet had never seen before were already sitting in the back of the vehicle.

While she hesitated, confused by the sight of the unexpected fourth member of their group, Rigg caught up with her, and firmly opened the front passenger door so that she had no option but to get in.

As he walked round to the driver's door Trixie greeted her enthusiastically, and introduced her companion.

'Harriet, this is Jonathan Walker. He's just started working for Rigg, and as yet he doesn't know very many people up here. He's only just down from Oxford, and he's been telling me all about it.'

Jonathan Walker shook Harriet's hand warmly as Trixie introduced them.

Listening to the flow of chatter coming from the back seat as Rigg drove them to their destination, Harriet couldn't help contrasting it with their silence.

Jonathan Walker seemed a pleasant young man, who Harriet quickly learned was very enthusiastic about his first job, and who seemed to be settling very happily into his new environment.

He was in rented accommodation in a small village not far from the factory, Harriet was told, and this was not the first time he and Trixie had met.

It had not occurred to her that they were going to be a foursome, and somehow or other this knowledge lent the evening an added intimacy, one that made her feel intensely conscious of Rigg seated at her side.

Both men were in evening dress, and from what she could see of it Trixie appeared to be wearing a very pretty dress in vivid blue and black, with a skirt not unlike her own although, instead of her sedate taffeta, Trixie's appeared to be black net spotted with bright blue dots.

She was also wearing her mother's pearls, and although she grumbled half-heartedly about being denied the all-night disco party with which Eva was going to celebrate her coming-of-age she didn't seem overly concerned that such an event was not for her.

It took them almost three-quarters of an hour to reach their destination, a country house set in what Harriet suspected would prove in daylight to be magnificent gardens.

Rigg was able to park close enough to the door for them all to be able to go in together. As Trixie fell into step with Jonathan, tucking her hand companionably through his arm, Harriet felt obliged to walk alongside Rigg, but while ahead of them Jonathan and Trixie walked companionably together, their steps matching, their heads close together, Harriet deliberately ensured that there was a couple of feet between herself and Rigg.

As they walked silently towards the warmly lit entrance to the hotel, Harriet couldn't help wondering what sort of torment she had let herself in for during the evening ahead.

CHAPTER EIGHT

HARRIET soon knew the evening would be painful. Once she and Trixie had handed over their coats they were escorted into a discreetly luxurious room where they were told they would be served with pre-dinner drinks.

The room had no bar, just some cleverly organised groups of chairs and sofas around tables, all of them positioned so that it was possible for their occupants to see and enjoy the warmth of the huge log fire burning in the fireplace.

The room was dimly lit, its décor a rich mingling of colours which added to its aura of warmth and comfort.

A waiter very quickly appeared with a hand-written list of the cocktails available.

Harriet repressed a small smile as Trixie predictably chose one more heavily laced with fruit than alcohol. She herself opted for Perrier water. They would probably be drinking wine with the meal and she had no wish to take any unnecessary risk with her self-control. Her stomach lurched protestingly as she remembered what two glasses of wine at the Vicarage party had already so insanely prompted her to do.

Rigg also decided on Perrier, while Jonathan very gallantly joined Trixie in her exotic choice.

Trixie wasn't shy as Harriet herself had been when younger, and chattered naturally and easily with Jonathan, questioning him about his home and his friends, apparently not in the least disturbed to discover that he had a girlfriend who was still at Oxford.

'Your uncle tells me that you yourself hope to go on to university,' Harriet heard Jonathan saying to her.

'Yes, but I doubt that I'll get to Oxford,' Trixie told him, grimacing a little. 'Both Dad and Rigg were up at Magdalen, so I rather feel as though I'm letting the side down a bit.'

Jonathan turned to Rigg and started asking him about his own university career, and while they were talking Trixie leaned across to Harriet.

'I love your dress,' she said admiringly. 'Did you buy it in London?'

Instantly Harriet felt the heat rise up under her skin. Rigg wasn't even listening to them, never mind looking at her, and yet she was acutely conscious of him as she said jerkily, 'No...no, I didn't.'

She was praying that Trixie wouldn't ask her where she had got it and when, and breathed out a thankful sigh of relief when the waiter arrived with their drinks and Trixie was distracted from questioning her further.

The hotel served a banquet-style dinner, Rigg informed them, rather than offering an *à la carte* menu, and within minutes of their own arrival, the cocktail bar filled up with other diners.

At eight-thirty the head waiter entered the room and announced that dinner was about to be served, and everyone started to move towards the double doors which had been flung open to reveal the dining-room beyond.

This room had tall windows all along one wall looking out across an illuminated terrace.

'In the summer they open the french windows so that people can stroll along the terrace,' Rigg informed Harriet.

Somehow or other they had once again formed two pairs, and as the head waiter indicated which was their table, Harriet felt Rigg place his hand beneath her arm, politely guiding her towards it.

Even through the thick velvet of her sleeve his touch burned her skin so that heat washed through her, making her flinch back automatically.

Immediately his hand was withdrawn, his mouth drawing into a hard, remote line as he stepped back from her.

Each table had its own handwritten menu, but Harriet couldn't share in Trixie's enthusiasm for the dishes listed. The last thing she felt like doing was eating, but this was a very special occasion for Trixie and she could not bear to spoil it for her. So, despite the protests of her turbulent stomach, she forced down every mouthful as course succeeded course.

Trixie at least was enjoying herself, Harriet observed with relief, as she herself finally refused any cheese. It seemed that although Jonathan was going home for Christmas, when he returned he would be bringing his girlfriend and his sister back with him. After a quick, enquiring look at Rigg, he suggested that Trixie might like to show them something of the countryside.

Was this why Rigg had invited Jonathan to join them? Harriet wondered. Because he considered her a more suitable friend for Trixie than Eva Soames?

If so, Harriet couldn't blame him. Trixie had already divulged to her that, unlike her, Eva was not intending to go on to university, but that once she had taken her A levels she was going to look for a job, and Harriet sensed this was another reason why Rigg did not wish Trixie to come too much under the influence of Eva and her mother.

The meal seemed interminable. Already Harriet was desperate to leave. With every second that passed she became more aware of Rigg and not less, more tense and on edge instead of more relaxed.

After the coffee had been served it was announced that there would be dancing in the ballroom for those who wished to avail themselves of this facility.

Immediately Trixie sprang up, her eyes sparkling, as she tugged impatiently at Rigg's sleeve.

'Come on, I'm dying to dance,' she told him, but Rigg restrained her with a few firm words.

'Harriet hasn't finished her coffee yet, Trixie.'

Quickly Harriet pushed the rich liquid away from her, announcing that she wasn't going to drink it. The last thing she wanted to do was to prolong the evening, but it was Trixie's birthday and so, forcing a smile to her face, she got to her feet.

The effort of smiling and talking had already made her face muscles ache with tension. Rigg had hardly spoken to her throughout the entire meal.

His attitude only confirmed what she already knew: that her presence was unwelcome to him. And yet when she stood up he rose too, and when they made their way to the ballroom, which was on the upper floor and reached via an elegant return staircase, he immediately placed his hand beneath her arm.

Even so, despite the outward intimacy of his gesture there was almost a foot of space between them as they went up the stairs. It was different for Trixie and Jonathan, who were several steps ahead of them, their bodies touching, their heads inclined towards one another as they talked.

Their silence was like the space that separated them, Harriet reflected miserably. It was infected by the stupidity of her behaviour last week. If she hadn't over-reacted like that, she and Rigg might almost have become friends.

She had begun to sense in him a reaching out towards her, a desire to share with her his concern for Trixie and a need to discuss his problems with a fellow adult. But now all that was gone, and the face she could see in profile was the same stern, withdrawn one she remembered from their first meeting. Oddly there was also a trace of that same anger in it. She could feel it pulsing through his body almost as if he fought to keep it under control.

She could have had his friendship, but now all she had was his anger and his resentment. Did he fear that she was stupid enough to weave some idiotic romantic fantasy around that one kiss? Did he think she didn't have the intelligence to know the *truth*?

She was glad when the top of the stairs was reached so that she could move firmly away from him.

For some reason her withdrawal from him made his mouth tighten and fierce sparks of molten gold ignite his eyes. She blinked a little, half transfixed by the heat in them. A heat that seemed to ignite a slow burn of sensation deep within her own body.

The knowledge that he could affect her so intensely both emotionally and physically frightened her, but it was only when Trixie turned to call to them, 'Come on, you two,' that she was able to break free of the magnetic spell of his gaze and follow the younger girl towards the ballroom.

The room was already busy with couples seating themselves at the small tables around the edge of the dance-floor, confirming Harriet's earlier impression that the hotel was well patronised.

The other women, the majority of whom were around her own age rather than Trixie's, were all so smartly dressed that she knew that her black velvet skirt would have looked shabby and out of place.

There were several large parties comprising what looked like family groups with younger members around Trixie's age, and the music played by the band was obviously geared to cover all tastes.

Trixie danced enthusiastically, first with her uncle and then later with Jonathan, after Jonathan had politely insisted on partnering Harriet.

He was a very pleasant young man, who obviously thought a good deal of his employer, and who was equally obviously a little lonely in his new environment so far away from his friends and family, and Harriet suspected that Rigg's motives in inviting him to join them had been as much for Jonathan's benefit as Trixie's.

Trixie certainly didn't lack for partners. A tall, ungainly boy with a family party came over and asked her to dance. Harriet estimated that he was probably the same age as Trixie, although from the almost maternal way she treated him it was plain that Trixie considered him immature.

It was after he had returned to their table, stammering his thanks and blushing painfully, that Trixie turned to Rigg and announced, 'Rigg, you haven't danced with Harriet yet.'

And before Harriet could say anything, Rigg stood up.

'An omission I was just about to remedy,' he said calmly, 'if Harriet will allow me.'

Impossible for her to refuse, and equally impossible for Rigg not to have asked her, Harriet recognised bleakly as she stood up.

Of course he didn't want to dance with her, but Trixie had really given him no option.

To her horror as he led her on to the floor, the tempo of the music changed, the lights dimming as the band started to play a sultry, slow number, which caused the other dancers to move closer together as they swayed intimately to the music.

It was music for lovers to dance to, Harriet recognised numbly, instinctively increasing the distance between them as Rigg turned to take hold of her.

'What's wrong?' he asked tersely as she held herself aloof from him.

'I . . . we can't dance to this.' Her face burned as she said the words.

She saw his mouth tighten, either in impatience or irritation but she couldn't tell which, and then he was giving her an angry, almost intimidating look.

'Well, we can hardly go back to the table, can we?'

And then before she could reply he had pulled her into his arms and was holding her unbearably close to his body as he moved in time to the music.

He was a good dancer, and had the circumstances been different the sensation of being held so close to him, of moving so intimately with him would have had her in seventh heaven. As it was she had to lock every muscle to prevent her traitorous flesh from melting against him while her arms, unlike those of the other female dancers, were braced stiffly between them, her hands flat against his shoulders as she tried to preserve some space between them.

Rigg seemed completely unaware of her tension. No doubt he was used to dancing in such intimacy, she told herself savagely. He certainly didn't seem to be aware of how easy it would be for her, in her present vulnerable state, to misconstrue the way he was holding her, his arms around her, one hand resting low down in the small of her back, the other holding her so that his fingers brushed the nape of her neck beneath her hair.

The effort of keeping her muscles locked was beginning to tell on her. As they moved across the floor towards the french windows Harriet felt the beginnings of an inward tremble in her over-tense body.

It was darker on this side of the ballroom, with one set of french windows open, revealing a long balcony. As they approached the darkness of the open windows, the trembling which had been internal suddenly exploded past her self-control, and there was nothing she could do to stop the convulsive and betraying shudders that seized her.

For one second it seemed as though Rigg's hold on her tightened, and then, just as she was telling herself she was imagining it, he deliberately loosened his grip on her, stepping back from her, so that they were dancing with at least six inches of space between them.

The musicians had started playing a second number, as sultry and intimate as the first, and as it began Harriet waited for Rigg to release her completely and return her to their table, his duty done. But to her surprise he didn't.

Suddenly it was all too much for her; the strain on her emotions and her nerves overwhelmed her, so that in the protective shadows she pulled away from him and said shakily, 'Look, let's go back, shall we? It's obvious that you don't want to dance with me.'

Oh, God, why had she said that, like a petulant child begging for reassurance? Why had she not simply said that she was tired, or that she thought Trixie would like to dance with him? Why come out with a remark like that?

She was already starting to walk away from him when he caught hold of her arm, and held on to it, saying harshly, 'My God, that's good. Me not want to dance with you. What the hell gives you that idea?'

The question baffled her almost as much as the anger she could sense emanating from him.

All evening she had been conscious of this anger, divining that it was directed against her, and she thought she knew why. Well, it was not her fault that she was here. And if he thought for one moment that she was going to embarrass them both by reading too much into a kiss which had got out of hand...

'You haven't answered me, Harriet,' he reminded her harshly. 'You say it's obvious I don't want to dance with you. I rather thought the boot was on the other foot, but no matter. *Why* is it so obvious that I don't want you as my partner?'

What had possessed her to initiate this conversation? She, who had always been so cautious and careful, was now quite deliberately and wantonly playing with fire.

He was bitterly angry, furious in fact, and perhaps he had every right to be. She had behaved stupidly.

Holding up her head, she said huskily, 'Look at the other dancers... This music is for...for lovers.' Her heart twisted painfully inside her. 'I—we...'

'For lovers. Which we aren't, as you were at great pains to make clear by keeping such distance between us as you could.'

The bitterness in his voice stunned her into saying unwisely, 'You did the same. Just now, before we stopped dancing, you——'

He swore suddenly under his breath, startling her. She had never heard him swear before, not even that first night they had met when she had refused to help him.

'Do you really want to know why I did that?' he demanded savagely. 'Well, then, come here and let me show you.'

And before she could stop him, he had pulled her back into his arms and was moulding her against his body.

She was unprepared for his actions, and it was too late for her to stop him, too late to force some space between them without physically struggling against him.

Even through the velvet of her dress she could feel the heat coming off his body. Her heart was thudding erratically, or was it his heartbeat she could feel? She felt dizzy, disorientated, a fierce surge of need pulsing through her veins. Her breasts were pressed hard against his chest, and, as he moved them both in a deliberately sensual response to the music, the sensation of his body against her own caused her nipples to harden and ache tormentingly.

'*This* is why I put some distance between us,' Rigg said grimly in her ear, as his hands swept down over her back moulding her against him so that there could be no way she was not made aware of the hard arousal of his body.

And even then he didn't relax his hold on her, but reinforced her awareness of his sexual arousal by moving against her so deliberately and erotically that she stared up at him with dazed, disbelieving eyes.

'Shocked?' he asked acidly. 'Why? Aren't I permitted to have all the normal male responses to a woman I find desirable? Or it is because you think such tangible evidence of them ought to be kept for the bedroom? Physical desire is an inconvenient thing, isn't it? Just when we think we've reached the age where we can control it, rather than it control us, it goes and makes a mockery of our self-conceit. *This* is why I put some distance between us, Harriet...because you'd already made it plain how distasteful you found me as a man, and I didn't want to embarrass us both further by——'

'I don't find you distasteful,' Harriet interrupted him, stumbling to a halt. 'You're the one who doesn't want me...'

There was a moment's hiatus, and then Rigg said shakily, 'My God, if we were anywhere but here—anywhere with the slightest pretensions to privacy—I'd shake you for——' He broke off as he felt the tension ease from her in a soft laugh, and his hands left her body to frame her face as he looked down into her eyes.

'What did you think I was going to say?' he asked huskily. 'That I'd *show* you how wrong you are?'

Her face gave her away.

'I'd do that as well,' he told her thickly. 'My God, Harriet, have you any idea of how much I want you? Here...now...this minute.'

He groaned and she saw the tension in his face; felt it in his body.

'All week I've been thinking about you... wanting...but you've been so cold towards me.' He was frowning now.

The dance had come to an end, but neither of them were aware of it until suddenly the lights came back on, making them both blink.

'We can't discuss this here. I need to see you alone so that we can talk.'

'Tomorrow?' Harriet hazarded uncertainly. 'Or next week when Trixie is back at school?'

Rigg shook his head.

'No...tonight. Can I come round and see you later, after I've dropped Jonathan off and taken Trixie home? Only to talk,' he added softly.

And, shockingly, inside her a pulse flared and ached, telling her how much she wanted to share far more with him than mere conversation.

'Yes...yes, all right,' she agreed, firmly ignoring the shocked voice inside her that said that this was the utmost folly.

Rigg wanted her.

For the rest of the evening, she felt as though she were floating several feet off the ground. While the others talked and danced she lived over and over again those seconds in Rigg's arms, when he had made her so forcefully and intimately aware that he desired her, and each time she did her own flesh ached and tingled in sensual reaction to her thoughts.

It was gone one o'clock when they eventually left. This time, as they walked out to the car, there was no distance separating her from Rigg, and when he leaned across from his own seat to fasten her seatbelt for her the sensation of his warm breath against her skin, and his hands brushing her body, sent fierce pulses rocketing through her.

As he moved away from her his hand brushed accidentally against her breast. Harriet heard his indrawn breath and knew what had caused it. She was glad of the darkness inside the Range Rover, to conceal both her flush and the fact that beneath the velvet bodice of her dress her breasts strained, eagerly desirous of his touch, her nipples hard and erect, their arousal clearly outlined beneath the velvet. It was this that had caused Rigg to check and half lean back to her, and she knew that had they been alone, nothing could have stopped him from cupping her wanton flesh with his hands and exploring the eagerness with which it flaunted its anticipation of his touch. Perhaps not just with his hands but with his mouth as well.

A long shudder ripped through her. How could she know so intensely the pleasure she would feel when his mouth touched her there, when she had never known the intimacy of such a caress? How could she know how eagerly her body would respond to him?

This time the silence in which she sat at Rigg's side was far different from the silence she had known earlier. This silence was filled with anticipation and excitement, with exhilaration and perhaps just a little touch of fear. After all, this was completely new territory for her, but, strangely, she had no fear that Rigg would find it odd or unacceptable that he would be her first lover.

They dropped Jonathan off first at his lodgings in Hawick, and when Trixie sleepily refused Harriet's offer to join her in the back she remained where she was, enjoying the nerve-tingling pleasure of being close to Rigg.

Once they reached her cottage, he walked with her to her front door and took the key from her to open it for her, but he didn't touch her and then, as though he knew what she was thinking, he said groaningly, 'I daren't... If I touch you now I won't be able to stop. Wait for me, won't you? I shouldn't be too long.'

For several minutes after he had gone she simply stood in the middle of her kitchen, staring into space, and then as her clock struck the half-hour she was galvanised into action. She would light a fire in the sitting-room so that they could talk in comfort . . . but first she'd have to change her dress unless she wanted to risk getting coal dust on it.

How much time did she have? She would have to hurry.

CHAPTER NINE

ONE half-hour passed and then another; the fire burned down and had to be restoked. Where was Rigg? Why was he taking so long?

Harriet waited until three o'clock before admitting that he wasn't going to appear, and then slowly dragged herself upstairs to bed.

It had all been a dream...a chimera. She had imagined the whole thing. He didn't want her at all. It had just been a cruel trick to make fun of her, she told herself sickly as she climbed into bed. He had just been amusing himself at her expense.

Logically she knew she was wrong, but then logically if he had meant what he had said he would be here with her now. He hadn't even telephoned her. She looked wistfully at the telephone and almost reached for the receiver, only her pride stopping her from picking it up and dialling his number.

Nearly an hour later, just when she was on the verge of falling asleep, she heard the car.

There was no time to get dressed, only to pull on her old shabby dressing-gown over her nightdress and run downstairs in her bare feet to let him in.

He was frowning as he stepped into the hallway, and as he looked at her Harriet acknowledged how little she really knew about him. A misogynist Trixie had called him when she had explained about how he had been rejected by his fiancée.

Suddenly Harriet was acutely conscious of how he might misconstrue her appearance, and the fact that she was so obviously undressed and ready for bed.

'I thought you weren't coming, so I went to bed,' she told him hastily. 'Your Range Rover woke me.'

'I'm sorry. Perhaps I shouldn't have come. It is late, but there was a phone call just as I was coming out. My agent in the States wanted to talk to me about a large order he'd been given. It's a new venture for us, selling over there.'

The tired shrug of his shoulders said so much, impelling Harriet to reply softly, 'This could have waited.'

He smiled then, a smile that mocked himself rather than her as he told her, 'Maybe it could, but I could not.'

Without thinking about what she was doing, she took a step towards him at the same moment as he moved towards her, and walked straight into his arms.

As they closed around her, she just had time to be surprised by the racing unsteadiness of his heartbeat before he kissed her. Not tentatively as he had done on Sunday but deeply and intensely—a man claiming what he already knew to be his.

Her bones turned weak and molten beneath the searing heat of pleasure that licked through her. Why had she never known before that it was possible to feel like this? Just by being kissed?

She made a soft verbal protest at her own insanity, and instantly Rigg took advantage of it, his tongue probing past her parted lips, exploring, seeking, thrilling her senses into a physical heightening that sharpened into an aching pulse.

His hands slid into her hair, angling her head so that he could deepen the kiss so that it was no longer a mere meeting of lips and tongues but an intimate acknowledgement of his need to possess her body in the same way that he was possessing her mouth.

Her arms around him, her body straining eagerly against his, Harriet shuddered under the impact of the savage pleasure that racked her as his hand slid down her back, pressing her into his body so that she could feel how much he wanted her. Every movement of his body against hers reinforced that wanting, making her ache to appease it, and yet he had come here merely to talk.

As though he too was suddenly aware of what they were inviting, he lifted his mouth from hers, and drew back slightly from her. Although he still held her, his hands firm and warm on her body, his touch was comforting rather than demanding.

'You make me react like a boy of seventeen, not a man of thirty-eight,' he told her rawly. 'I don't normally go around behaving like this, you know.'

Although he said it almost ruefully, Harriet recognised the serious note underlying the words.

'Neither do I,' she admitted. 'In fact——'

She gave a tiny shiver and, noticing it, Rigg let go of her, taking hold of her hand.

'It's cold in here. You're shivering.'

She had been shivering when he kissed her, but not with cold, and the gap between her own knowledge and his suddenly yawned a little frighteningly at her feet, as she recognised the gulf in their sexual experience.

'The sitting-room fire should still be warm. We can talk in there...'

He held her hand as she reached for the door, lacing his fingers with hers in a way that made her heart thud frantically when his fingers brushed against hers. Such a brief physical intimacy and yet in its own way as erotic as his earlier kiss.

The fire was still in, and Rigg soon had it burning up brightly again as he added more logs to its embers.

A pleasant scent of woodsmoke filled the room, and the deep silence of the night surrounded them. In such an atmosphere what she ought to be feeling was a deep sense of peace, but what she was feeling was a fierce surge of awareness mingled with an almost uncontrollable ache of need. If he touched her again...

But he didn't. He settled himself in the chair opposite her own as he began, without preamble, 'I can't pretend that this hasn't come as something of a surprise to me. I thought the days were long since gone when I was liable to react to a woman—any woman—the way I've reacted to you.'

Harriet moved uneasily in her chair. This wasn't what she wanted to hear, this flat, almost unwilling admission of physical desire. No, what she wanted was an impassioned declaration of love; she *wanted* to hear him say that his need was emotional as well as physical... she *wanted* him to say the words that would free her to admit her own feelings.

But he wasn't... Suddenly she felt chilled and desolate. Rigg was talking about reaction, just when she wanted to hear him talking about love.

She got up from her chair and moved restlessly around the room while he watched, a frown etched between his eyes. She couldn't look at him. She knew if she did she would break down completely and tell him everything she was feeling.

Instead she said shakily, 'I don't think this is a good idea, Rigg. I accept that you—that you want me...'

'But?' he challenged harshly, hearing the doubts in her voice.

Harriet shook her head, unable to trust her voice for several seconds. When she had herself under sufficient control to speak, she said unevenly, 'I'm frightened, Rigg. I'm not used to this kind of thing. I——'

He didn't let her go on any further, interrupting savagely, 'Don't you think it's exactly the same for me? For God's sake, I'm thirty-eight years old, long past the age when I anticipated experiencing something like this.'

He too was on his feet now, pacing the room like a caged hunting cat. She could almost see the sparks of anger and irritation coming off him.

'It's knocked me right off my feet. Falling in love virtually at first sight.' He shook his head, his back to her as Harriet absorbed the wonder of what he had said. Falling in love...he loved her. It wasn't just physical desire he felt for her.

'I thought I was going out of my mind, suffering from some form of middle-aged madness——'

'But you *can't* love me,' Harriet protested uncertainly, too bemused to conceal what she was feeling.

He swung round and stared at her, his eyes and voice flat.

'Oh, but I do,' he told her softly.

Her colour rose, a fierce pulse beating urgently through her body.

'Rigg...'

'Look, let's stop trying to analyse it, shall we, and just let ourselves enjoy the gift we've been given? Let's just go with the flow.'

'To wherever it takes us,' Harriet said as lightly as she could, searching his face.

There was a small pause, and then Rigg said abruptly, 'We already know where it's taking us.'

She gave him a tremulous smile.

'You may do, Rigg, but I'm not wise to this kind of thing.'

'And you think I am,' he derided. 'Since Trixie's arrival in my life, I've virtually been celibate. There's nothing like the responsibility of bringing up a teenage girl for repressing sexual desire. Only this is something that can't be repressed or controlled. This is something different...something special.' He reached for her, his fingers twining with hers, sending sharp spears of sexual tension darting through her body.

'Something neither of us has experienced for a long time,' he added softly.

'Something I've *never* experienced before,' Harriet told him shakily, and then admitted, 'It terrifies me, Rigg. I'm not used to feeling like this... There's never been anyone in my life before who has made me feel this way and it's not just that...' Her head dipped a little, and she swallowed, suddenly nervous. 'I know it must sound strange in this day and age, but I haven't had any previous lovers.'

When she looked up at him he was smiling gently at her, but beneath his smile she could see that her admission had pleased some elemental male corner of his psyche, and her breath caught in her throat as she read in his eyes his pleasure in knowing that what they would share would for her be her first experience of passion.

Yet still she felt nervous, unsure, wanting to make it clear to him that for her this was no casual affair, and yet too proud, too reserved to ask him for the words of reassurance she craved.

'I don't have the experience to cope with——' Rejection, she had been about to say, but at the last moment she changed her mind and instead said lamely, 'With this kind of thing.'

'This is something no amount of experience ever prepares you for,' Rigg told her, his thumb smoothing the vulnerable inner flesh of her wrist and registering its rapid pulse.

'I love you, and I want you. I want to take hold of you right now this minute and show you how I feel. I want to touch your body and to see in your eyes that I'm touching your heart at the same time. I want to watch your eyes cloud with passion, at the same time as I feel your body move beneath my hands. I want to learn by touch each contour of your skin, the swell of your breasts, the curve of your belly, the satin softness of your thighs and then I want to feel them all again beneath my mouth.'

He heard the sound she tried to suppress and stopped.

As she listened to his flat, controlled voice delivering the words, her body ached with such an intensity of feeling that it was as though he were actually already touching her.

She tried not to utter the small betraying sound that rose in her throat, but he heard it and immediately tensed. His voice was suddenly raw and unsteady as he said roughly, 'Harriet,' and then she was in his arms.

He was kissing her as she had so often during the last week imagined him doing. The only difference was that the reality of his need far exceeded even the most erotic of her fantasies.

She made no protest when his hands slid beneath her dressing-gown and found the softness of her breasts. Her body wasn't a girl's, but her flesh was smooth and firm, and when his fingers tugged urgently at her ribbon in the neckline of her nightdress, so that he could release the bodice, she felt no embarrassment in the way he slid the fabric free of her skin so that he could gaze at the creamy fullness of her exposed breasts.

When he gently traced one blue vein to the rim of the smooth aureole of flesh beyond which her nipple peaked urgently and wantonly, she shuddered, unable to stop the quivering response his touch evoked.

Was it just her imagination, or were her breasts really swelling and straining towards him, begging for his touch? It was a completely new phenomenon for her, this fierce excitement of her pleasure, this wild yearning ache that possessed it like an alien force.

His thumb brushed across her nipple, a gentle, almost hesitant caress, but immediately her flesh felt the contact with the rough stimulation of his harder skin. It pulsed visibly in erotic response.

Dazed by the intensity of what she was feeling, Harriet stared at the slow, rhythmic movement of his thumb until even her breathing and her heartbeat mirrored its subtle rhythm. Until even the ache buried deep inside her throbbed in silent response to his touch.

'Rigg...' Her voice sounded cracked and splintered, and she wasn't sure herself if she was making a protest or a plea.

Rigg seemed to know, though.

He made a fierce sound deep in his throat, his hands lifting to curl into her hair, tilting her head backwards, his mouth causing a hot, wild tide of sensation to roar through her as he traced the length of her exposed throat, and then moved down until he was savaging the vulnerable cord that pulsed beneath her skin, making her twist and cry out against him.

He seemed to know exactly the moment her self-control broke, dropping down into a chair and taking her with him, first his hand finding her exposed breast and then his mouth.

When he drew fiercely on her flesh, she was pierced with the most elemental sensation she had ever known.

Her whole body arched convulsively in a need that was answered almost immediately by the hard warmth of his hand caressing her thigh and then moving higher until he was touching her where she most ached to be touched, drawing whimpers of mindless pleasure from her as his mouth tugged erotically on the sensitive pulsing of her breast and his hand against her body made her cry out to him that she wanted him.

After that there was no turning back, nor did she want there to be. Nature had taken over from reason and was driving her on, refusing to allow her time to think or reason.

This, nature told her, was what she had been designed for, what she had been born for; it was an elemental tide which there was no holding back, and plainly Rigg thought so too.

Naked and supine, she lay beneath him in front of the fire as he soothed the sharp immediacy of her need into a voluptuous welcoming of the intimate caresses of his hands and mouth.

This time she was free to study him in his nakedness as she had not been that first time they had met. This time there was no need for her to avert her eyes from the dark arrowing of hair bisecting his body in a narrow line which on that previous occasion had discreetly disappeared beneath the waistband of his briefs.

Now there was nothing to conceal from her the reality of his maleness, nor did he seem either embarrassed or amused by her hesitant reaction to him. Instead he seemed to know exactly what she was feeling as he took her hand and slowly and deliberately placed it on his body, uncurling her tense fingers and holding them under his own as he showed her that he was no more than human, and that her touch had the capacity to make him tremble and cry out just as his did for her.

After his earlier declaration of how much he needed her she had expected him to make love to her quickly and impatiently. She was confused by his slow and gentle seduction of her, his deliberate and gentle arousal of her body to the point where it shocked her by exploding into rhythmic pulses of shattering pleasure beneath the skilled touch of his hands, long before he actually entered her and showed her again, with the rhythmic drive of his body within her own, that same pleasure.

Then he explained softly, 'I didn't want to hurt you, but I can't always promise to be so gentle. You arouse me to a pitch I can't even begin to explain to you, Harriet...'

She shocked herself almost as much as she stunned him, when she demanded huskily, 'Show me, then... show me how much you want me.'

And later, exulting beneath the fierce compulsive thrust of his body within her own, she knew that this second time she was experiencing his true desire, and gave herself up rapturously to accommodating each powerful movement of his body, so that the quick convulsions of pleasure that seized her came as an unexpected extra pleasure to those he had already shown her.

Later, naked and sated, she lay in his arms, wishing they could stay like this together, shut away from the rest of the world... Alone, together. But already Rigg was moving away from her.

'I must go,' he was saying regretfully. 'There's nothing I want more than to stay here with you... to hold you through the night and have you wake up in my arms. But I'm afraid that it's just not possible.'

She watched him as he dressed, huddling into her own dressing-gown, cold now that he was leaving her, wanting to cry almost like a forlorn child, experiencing a deep intensity of depression that she couldn't understand.

Rigg seemed to, though. Bending down towards her, he cupped her head, turning it so that he could look into her eyes.

'Post-coital blues,' he told her softly, and then, dropping a gentle kiss on her mouth, he stood up.

Huskily he said, 'I've got to go into the factory tomorrow and check to see if we've got the stock for this American order, but just as soon as I can I'll ring you.'

Another kiss, a more lingering one this time that made her mouth tremble and cling weakly to his, and then he was gently disengaging himself from her and moving to the door.

It was almost six o'clock... How many hours before she could see him again?

She went upstairs to bed, her mind and her heart full of him. He had been a wonderful lover—kind, considerate, and then, when he knew that it was what she wanted too, more passionate than she had dreamed any man could be.

Already small bruises were beginning to darken her skin where he had marked her in his need. None of them were painful, but all of them reminded her of how he had made her feel, and as she fell asleep already she was aching for him again.

Neither of them had any form of protection to prevent a pregnancy, but she was reasonably sure that at such a time of the month it was unlikely that she would conceive. And even if she did...

She shuddered violently, imagining conceiving Rigg's child, her stomach convulsing on the pleasure the thought brought.

Rigg's child. Rigg. How much she loved him. But did he love her as intensely?

She hated the way the small maggot of doubt wormed its way into her mind, fighting to resist its insistent burrowing.

Of course he loved her. He had said so.

Yes, he had said so, but had he *meant* it? *Did* he love her in the way that she loved him? Did he want her permanently in his life? Did he want her as his wife, or simply as his lover?

Impossible now to sleep. She was taut with anxiety and fear, willing away the hours until Rigg telephoned her. Somehow it wasn't enough that he had made love to her with tenderness and love; she needed the words as well, needed to hear him say that he wanted her with him for always, that he wanted her in his life permanently, as his wife . . . as the mother of his children.

How long would it be before he telephoned? She tried mentally to calculate when she could expect his call. Not before mid-morning certainly, and possibly not even until lunchtime, depending on how long he was at the factory.

A long time...a lifetime. But somehow she would have to live through it.

CHAPTER TEN

MID-MORNING came and went without a telephone call from Rigg. Harriet comforted herself by reminding herself that mid-morning had been the earliest estimate of when he would contact her. Lunchtime was probably closer to the mark, and she made herself resist the impulse to pick up the receiver and ring the Hall.

At one o'clock the tension gripping her body was making her muscles ache; by two she was feeling physically sick beneath the burden of knowledge slowly creeping over her.

By three she knew the truth. Rigg wasn't going to telephone.

In less than twenty-four hours she had gone from despair to euphoria, through the full gamut of emotions from anguish to ecstasy, and now back to anguish again. Only this time the anguish was sharper, piercing her with fire-tipped arrows of rejection, self-contempt, loneliness and the knowledge that she loved where her love was not likely to be returned.

Desperately she tried to tell herself that there could be a straightforward reason why Rigg hadn't rung: another important telephone call, or a business matter. But sheer common sense refused to allow her to cling to such a frail piece of driftwood. Rigg hadn't telephoned because, like so many other men, in the cold light of day he was having second thoughts about promises implicit in the actions of the previous night.

She had thought herself sufficiently intelligent to know the difference between a man's desire and his love. A lifetime ago, as a teenager, she had been quick to discern what it was her youthful dates wanted from her when they pressed their clumsy kisses against her lips and tried to fumble beneath her sweater or blouse. But in the long years of her maturity she had grown so accustomed to thinking of herself as beyond being desired that that once-active self-protectiveness had deserted her.

And besides, she asked herself bitterly, if she was honest with herself, hadn't she needed and loved Rigg so much last night that she had been beyond questioning his motives in making love to her?

It was her fault and hers alone if she had deceived herself into believing that he loved her as she loved him.

By the time dusk fell she had abandoned her last frail hope that he might still get in touch with her.

Rigg was an astute man—a compassionate man, she would have said once. He must know what she was thinking, what she was feeling, what she was going through. There was only one interpretation to be placed on the fact that he hadn't contacted her, and that was that he was trying to tell her as bluntly as he could that what had happened between them was not something he wished to pursue.

And yet, despite the fact that he had not got in touch with her, despite her knowledge that emotionally he had rejected her, she found that she couldn't regret the fact that they had made love.

Had she been able to turn back the clock and have the last twenty-four hours over again she knew that she would not have given up a single heartbeat of the time she had spent in his arms.

Maybe he could not give her his love, but he had given her pleasure beyond any she had known could exist. He had given her pride and delight in her body and its ability to please him, and he had given her a deep awareness of the slow-running tide of her femininity and of the unexpected depths of her sensuality, things she had not known before that she possessed. And in his lovemaking he had shown her caring as well as desire. Was it his fault that she had hoped for so much more?

If he couldn't love her, perhaps after all it was for the best, this silence of his, the sharp, severing cut that wounded but did not maim. Perhaps he had not realised until last night how much she loved him. He had spoken of loving her, but perhaps his conception of that emotion was different from her own, or perhaps he had sensed her desire for commitment by him, and it was that which had made him withdraw from her. Whatever the case, she was hardly likely to learn the truth.

Later that night, as she prepared for bed, she acknowledged that the pain of losing Rigg so soon after she had known the rapture of being loved by him was something that wasn't going to conveniently disappear overnight. She knew already that this night was one she would spend sleepless, going over and over every word they had both said, everything they had done, searching for the smallest hint of a signpost she had missed that would have prepared her for this anguish.

If she had dreaded seeing Rigg before, it was nothing to what she felt now. Long before the grey dawn was breaking over the distant hills, she knew that the only way of ensuring that she did not see Rigg again was to put the cottage up for sale and move away from the district.

It told her much about her own vulnerability that the very thought brought tears to her eyes and made her feel alone in a way she had never experienced before. But her mind was made up. The cottage must be sold; she must find somewhere else to live.

At six o'clock she was up, sitting in her kitchen, her hands wrapped around the comforting warmth of a mug of freshly made coffee, but the fragrant liquid failed to give her its normal boost. She felt sick and shaky, disorientated, as though she was suffering from shock, which in a way she supposed that she was.

It seemed a long, long time before her clock struck nine and she was able to ring the agent she had bought the cottage from.

She could hear his surprise humming down the wire when she told him she wanted to put her home up for sale.

Harriet couldn't blame him for being surprised. She had been so enthusiastic about the cottage— so much in love with it and its situation.

Sensing his curiosity, she fibbed a little.

'I'm beginning to feel a bit cut off. The cottage is rather remote. I think I might be happier living closer to other people.'

'Well, I appreciate what you're saying,' the agent agreed. 'But I'm afraid I can't recommend that you try to sell now. Traditionally this isn't a good time of the year for selling; the cottage is remote and needs a very special type of buyer. Even with the improvements you've done, I doubt that you'd recoup what you've spent, were you to insist on trying to sell at this time of the year. In the spring, now...'

The spring. Harriet felt her heart leap as though she'd been given a reprieve from a death sentence. Her hand gripped the receiver tightly. Oh, God, how she ached to give in...to allow herself the fatal joy of staying. Fatal to her ability to recover from her hopeless love for Rigg, and not fair to either of them.

She must not weaken. If she stayed until spring, might she not stay forever, helplessly caught up in a downward spiral of weakness that allowed her to believe that by some miracle Rigg might one day look at her and love her?

No, she couldn't allow herself to do that.

Taking a deep breath, she said as firmly as she could, 'I don't want to wait until the spring. I'm prepared to take a loss on the sale.'

She could tell that the agent, an old-fashioned, cautious man, was concerned, but she overrode any further objections that he might make by adding hardily, 'Of course, if you'd rather I went to another agent——'

'No... no, of course not. I'm likely to be out of the office for the next few days. If I could make an appointment to come and see you, take measurements, that sort of thing, say on Friday morning?'

Harriet wanted to scream with impatience. Surely he already had details of the room sizes from when she had purchased the cottage, but she sensed that to try to drive him would only produce negative results. So she gave way and said she would see him on Friday.

Friday. Five long days away. Five long days in which to brood, in which to remember, in which to ache with longing for Rigg. In which she could masochistically enjoy the self-torment of walking into her small sitting-room, and remembering how he had made love to her there.

Unable to endure the thought of staying in the cottage, aching for Rigg, mourning what she had hoped they would share, she picked up her car keys, and, locking the cottage behind her, got into her car.

She spent the entire day driving around aimlessly, through tiny stone villages and large market towns, and along empty roads that wound up into the hills, barren now with the onset of winter. How many miles she travelled she had no idea, and although she told herself that she was searching the area, looking for somewhere she could move to, she knew that in reality what she was doing was trying to escape from the pain of knowing that Rigg did not return her love.

She stopped once at lunchtime in a small village, parking on the forecourt of a weathered pub, telling herself that she ought to have some lunch.

Once inside, the warmth and cosiness of the atmosphere overwhelmed her, and she left after only a single bite of the sandwiches she had ordered, unable to endure the companionship that everyone around her seemed to share. A couple sitting in an alcove by the huge roaring fire, deeply engrossed in one another and obviously lovers, had awakened such a pain inside her that she had to tense her body against its overwhelming recoil.

The girl who had served her watched her leave, frowning in concern over her white face and almost stumbling gait, stirred to pity for the anguish she had seen in her eyes.

By Wednesday her reflection in her mirror told Harriet that what she was suffering was taking its toll on her physically as well as emotionally.

She knew that she had lost weight, but to see that weight loss in the dramatic sharpening of the contours of her face, so that the reflection staring back at her seemed all eyes and sharp cheekbones, made her acknowledge that if she didn't want people to wonder what on earth was happening to her, she must try to pull herself together.

The problem was that, no matter how sensible she tried to be, she couldn't eat and she couldn't sleep. She had stopped listening for the telephone now. When it shrilled, suddenly splintering the silence late on Wednesday morning when she was supposed to be working but was in reality sitting staring into space, thinking, not of her characters, but of Rigg, she stared at it for several seconds as though its purpose were unfamiliar to her.

Eventually she got up and reached for the receiver, her movements those of a sleepwalker, or someone deeply under the influence of drugs.

She picked it up, frowning as she heard Trixie's quick, anxious voice.

'Harriet,' she was saying, 'Is that you? Oh, please, can you come round? I need your help desperately.' There was a sound suspiciously like a sob and then Trixie repeated anxiously, 'Harriet...'

The younger girl's obvious need galvanised her into action. Without stopping to waste time in asking questions, she said quickly, 'I'll come straight away, Trixie. I'll be about ten minutes.'

It took her exactly seven, and as she stopped her small car on the gravel outside the Hall's front door she was conscious of having driven more recklessly than she had perhaps ever done in her life before.

She had no idea what was wrong, but suspected that Trixie must have had some sort of confrontation with Rigg, probably over her friendship with Eva, and that she needed to talk it over with someone. There must be something badly wrong if she hadn't gone to school. It had been obvious from her voice that the younger girl was close to tears, and Harriet was not surprised when Trixie flung open the door and came running out of the house towards her.

'Oh, thank goodness you're here! Rigg said I wasn't to tell you, but I just didn't know who else to turn to. What with Mrs Arkwright and Tom being away—I've managed to get him upstairs now, and he's asleep. Well, at least, I think he's sleeping.'

Harriet stared at her.

'Oh, please, hurry,' Trixie implored her, taking hold of her arm. 'Harriet, I'm so worried about him... They said at the hospital that there might be some residual concussion... But they let him come home so I thought he was all right. But then, when we got inside, he just sort of collapsed.'

They were inside the hall now. Harriet didn't know which of them was shaking more, herself or Trixie.

'It was so awful,' Trixie told her. 'Waking up on Sunday morning and finding his note saying that he'd had to go into the factory, and then the police arriving and saying that there'd been an accident—that someone had tried to break into the factory, not expecting anyone to be there, and that Rigg had been injured trying to stop them. I wanted to telephone you then, but the police didn't give me time... And then, at the hospital, I had to wait for ages to see the doctor, and he wouldn't tell me anything apart from the fact that Rigg was unconscious.'

She shuddered, while Harriet listened to her tale in growing shock.

Rigg injured! Hurt... unconscious... lying motionless in a hospital bed, unable to get in touch with her. Unable to get in touch with her!

Abruptly she focused on Trixie, and demanded almost fiercely, 'Why didn't you ring me before now? Why?'

'Because Rigg wouldn't let me,' Trixie told her. 'He came round on Monday, and when they let me see him he asked me if you'd been in touch at all. When I said no, I asked him if he wanted me to let you know what had happened. He said no. He'd be furious with me if he knew you were here now,' Trixie added. 'But I just didn't know who else I could turn to... I was so frightened... He was supposed to be all right...'

Tears welled in her eyes, and Harriet, despite her own sick fear, tried to reassure her, saying huskily,

'Well, the first thing we must do is to call the doctor.'

A little to her surprise, Trixie seemed uneasy with her suggestion. She gnawed on her bottom lip and suggested, 'Hadn't you better see him first? I mean, he might have come round now...we might not need to bother the doctor.'

Harriet blinked a little in surprise.

'But, Trixie, if he's suffering from concussion it's *vitally* important that we let the doctor know.'

'He hated being in hospital,' Trixie told her inconsequentially. 'He was furious when they wouldn't let him come home straight away but kept him in for tests. I think we should wait a little while and see if he comes round. I feel so much better now that you're here, Harriet,' she added ingenuously. 'He was in such a furious mood when I went to pick him up. Not like his normal self at all.'

Unable to stop herself, Harriet asked unevenly, 'You said he told you not to get in touch with me. Did he say why?'

'Oh, something about not bothering you—about you having your own life. That sort of thing. I told him you wouldn't mind, but he just went off the deep end.'

Had he not wanted Trixie to get in touch with her because he had already decided that he didn't want her?

'I think we ought to call the doctor,' she said firmly. Then, seeing Trixie's stubborn face, she added more gently, 'If he *is* suffering from concussion, Trixie, we have to let the doctor know.'

'But maybe it isn't concussion. Maybe he just felt faint or something. Why don't you go up and see him? Please,' she begged.

Harriet looked helplessly at her.

'Trixie, I don't know the first thing about medical matters. I won't be able to tell whether he's concussed or not.'

'No, but I'd feel much better if you'd just *look* at him. He was in the bedroom when he collapsed. I managed to get him to the bed, but his left arm looks sort of funny.'

Seeing that Trixie wouldn't give her any peace until she had complied with her urgings, Harriet sighed.

'All right, but I want you to promise me that as soon as I've seen him you'll call the doctor, because if you won't, I shall.'

'OK,' Trixie told her sunnily. 'Come on, it's this way.'

The young had a remarkable facility for recovery, Harriet reflected as she followed Trixie upstairs. Not ten minutes ago, the younger girl had been in tears of panic and fear, and yet now she was smiling as happily as though not a thing were wrong.

She, though, had knots in her stomach nothing could unravel. Fear for Rigg overpowered her reluctance to intrude on his privacy, even if he himself, if unconscious, would be unaware of her presence.

He didn't want her in his life. He had made that plain, and she shrank from the added pain and humiliation of having him think she was so thick-skinned that she hadn't realised how he felt and, worse, that she was deliberately trying to force her way into his life.

'It's this room,' Trixie told her, pushing open a heavy oak door, and then holding it so that Harriet had to step past her into the room.

All she could see of Rigg was the outline of his fully clad body as he lay face down on the cover of the heavy four-poster bed.

As she automatically moved closer so that she could get a better look at him, she heard the door closing.

Turning her head, she started to speak to Trixie, and then frowned.

She was alone in the room, and as she stared in bewilderment at the closed door she heard a noise that sounded alarmingly like a key being turned in the lock.

Impossible, and yet she walked unsteadily towards the door and tried the handle. It was locked.

Had Trixie gone mad? What on *earth* was she trying to do? She twisted the door handle helplessly.

'Trixie, what are you doing?' she demanded.

No reply came from outside the door, but from the bed there was a soft cough and a drowsy, 'Trixie, I thought——'

As Harriet wheeled round she saw Rigg turn over and sit up.

'You,' he said thickly, quickly hiding his shock, so that his face held no expression at all.

'Trixie asked me to come,' she told him helplessly, unable to think of anything else to say. 'She told me you'd collapsed. She was worried you might be suffering from concussion.'

'Did she? And that brought you to my bedside, did it?'

He sounded angry, and more; he sounded bitterly derisive, so that the colour stung up under her skin as she guessed what he must be thinking, that she had seized on the excuse to force her presence on him.

'Trixie sounded distraught,' she told him huskily. 'I had no idea what was wrong... I thought perhaps she'd quarrelled with you.'

'And that brought you running... female solidarity? I thought I knew you, but I didn't know you at all, did I, Harriet?'

He was sitting up now on the edge of the bed, and, although she could see a strip of sticky plaster marking a slightly swollen area of one temple, there was no other visible evidence of anything wrong. Certainly he neither looked nor behaved like someone who had just collapsed with concussion. He was far too alert.

The suspicion that Trixie had deliberately tricked her into coming here—that she had deliberately coaxed her up here to Rigg's room and locked her in with him—began to filter through her shock.

'I thought you were that rare prize among your sex,' Rigg was continuing bitterly. 'A woman who preferred to live her life alone rather than share it with a man to whom she couldn't give her whole heart. I couldn't believe my luck in finding you... I *shouldn't* have believed it, should I? I'd fallen in love with a mirage. With a woman who didn't exist. The days are long gone when anyone but a fool believes that a woman in her thirties is unattached for any reason other than that it's her own choice.

My mistake was in believing that your reason was one of the *heart* when in reality it's your freedom that matters most in your life, not your emotions.'

Harriet stared at him, unable to take in what he was saying. His accusations, bitter and full of pain, were so totally at odds with everything she had told herself he would be feeling that it took her several minutes to accept what she was hearing.

Her heart was thudding so loudly that she felt sure he must be able to hear it. She took a step closer to the bed, and to him, and then another.

Everything in her shrank from what she was doing, but something still impelled her onward. She had never in her whole life ever dared to make any kind of claim on another human being, not for their understanding, not for their support, and certainly not for their love. But that was what she was going to do now, and nothing was going to stop her.

'You promised you'd phone me,' she told him unsteadily. 'I waited——'

He was frowning at her. He didn't let her finish, but broke in explosively, 'And so I did, damn you. Or at least, I asked them at the hospital to ring you, and let you know what had happened. I even gave them your number, 872302.'

Harriet felt that if she didn't stand still exactly where she was, if she dared to lift her foot off the ground, she would float right up to the ceiling.

Carefully, as though she were frightened of breaking something, she corrected him quietly.

'No, it's 872303.'

For a moment they stared at one another.

Then Rigg said harshly, 'But you didn't make any attempt to get in touch. I asked Trixie if you'd rung.'

'How *could* I?' Harriet challenged him. 'Your last words to me were that you'd be in touch. I could think of only one reason why you didn't.'

'And that was?' he asked her.

'I thought you'd changed your mind... or even perhaps realised that I wanted more from you than you wanted to give.'

There was a sharp silence and then he demanded, visibly furious, 'You thought I'd deliberately seduced you, and that I was going to leave you flat?'

Harriet winced at the acidity in his voice.

Put like that it sounded so brutal—made him sound so callous and cruel.

'After how we'd been together... you actually thought——'

Harriet hung her head, unable to speak.

'Even if I hadn't already told you I loved you, even if the way I felt about you hadn't been implicit in the way we made love, surely you knew that common decency must have made me check that, if nothing else, you weren't pregnant?'

Harriet hadn't even considered that.

'You actually thought I'd make love to you and then walk out of your life——'

'I thought that you might not have realised until we had made love just how much I loved you, and that I wanted a permanent place in your life, not a temporary one,' Harriet told him bravely. 'And then, when you didn't get in touch——'

'Oh, my God,' Rigg said roughly.

His head was in his hands, but suddenly he looked up at her and said unsteadily, 'Come here.'

She went to him willingly, trembling a little with reaction as he stood up and took hold of her.

'I love you,' he told her rawly. 'I want to share the rest of my life with you... I want you as my wife... as the mother of my children. I want you in all the ways there are, Harriet, and then some more. If I didn't tell you all those things when I made love to you, then I'm sorry. But they were there. I can't begin to tell you how it felt when I came round in that damned hospital and found that you hadn't been in touch. I'd been so sure that the first thing I'd see when I opened my eyes would be you... and then Trixie, blast her, had to keep going on about letting you know... rubbing salt in the wound. I thought you did know.'

He kissed her once gently, and then a second time far less gently.

As she eased herself away from him, she asked huskily, 'Should you be doing this? After your collapse?'

'What collapse?'

'Trixie rang me in an absolute panic, begging me to come over. When I got here, she explained to me about your being attacked, and then said you'd collapsed up here. I thought you must be concussed. I wanted to get the doctor, but she wouldn't let me.'

'I'm not surprised,' Rigg told her grimly. 'I didn't collapse at all. They'd filled me with some kind of pain-killer in the hospital that made me feel drowsy, and they said before I left that the best way to get rid of it was to sleep it off. The only thing was that it was doing nothing at all to alleviate the kind of pain losing you was causing me.'

Glancing at the locked door, Harriet asked him thoughtfully, 'Does Trixie know... about us?'

'I should think so. I was rambling my head off while I was in hospital. I suspect the entire area knows by now how much I love you...'

Then he saw the way she looked at the door.

'What's wrong?' he asked her quickly.

When she explained she half expected him to be annoyed at the way Trixie had manipulated them both, but instead he laughed.

It said much about his nature that he could take his niece's interference so well, Harriet thought, acknowledging that if perhaps she had studied the man more, and her own insecurities less, she would not have allowed herself to believe that he didn't care.

'When can we be married?' he asked her. His lips were now against her ear. 'It had better be soon... I'm too old for midnight expeditions to your cottage and, besides, I want to wake up in the morning with you beside me instead of alone.'

'Before Christmas,' Harriet suggested, 'but with one proviso.'

'Anything,' Rigg said, so fervently that she laughed.

'A skiing honeymoon, after Christmas.'

He looked surprised.

'I didn't know you were a keen skier?'

'I'm not,' she told him with a grin, 'but I think Trixie deserves some sort of consolation prize for all her hard work, don't you?'

They were still laughing ten minutes later, when Trixie cautiously unlocked the door and came in carrying a tray with a bottle of champagne on it and three glasses, and a white handkerchief tied to a large spoon.

Half an hour later, the champagne drunk and the wedding date set, she told them astringently, 'Well, thank goodness that's all settled. Honestly, the pair of you were behaving like a couple of kids. Jonathan and I could both see on Saturday how it was with you.'

When she had gone, Harriet remembered something she still had to ask Rigg.

'The girl you were going to marry...'

He looked perplexed, and Harriet told him hesitantly how Trixie had told her that he had been left at the altar, and how it had affected him.

To her surprise he laughed.

'Oh, that. The engagement was broken by mutual consent, without any pangs of regret on either side. How on earth Trixie got hold of the idea I ever suffered unrequited love, I've no idea... I was too young to know the difference between love and infatuation when we got engaged but luckily we both grew up enough in time to recognise that what we had had was not meant to be permanent.

'I've only ever loved one woman,' he told her softly, 'and that's you.'

On Christmas Day Harriet and Rigg had been married exactly one week. After church in the morning, they drove back to the house along frost-whitened roads, to the welcome heat of a huge log fire, burning cheerily in the drawing-room.

More presents than Harriet thought she had ever seen in her life were heaped beneath the huge tree she and Rigg and Trixie had chosen together.

They had saved their surprise present for Trixie until last. When they handed her the envelope, she stared at it and then opened it in silence, a beatific smile illuminating her face when she saw what was inside it.

'You're taking me with you,' she crowed, running over to them and hugging them both tightly.

'Well, Harriet felt you deserved some reward for your meddling,' Rigg told her. 'And since I couldn't agree to your going skiing with Eva Soames, we thought that this might be a form of compensation.'

'Harriet, you're the best!' Trixie told her new aunt magnanimously.

Under his breath Rigg said softly to his new wife, 'Sentiments with which I heartily concur, Mrs Matthews.'

This August, don't miss an exclusive
two-in-one collection of earlier love stories

MAN
WITH A PAST

TRUE COLORS

by one of today's hottest
romance authors,

Jayne Ann Krentz

Now, two of Jayne Ann Krentz's most loved books are
available together in this special edition that new and
longtime fans will want to add to their bookshelves.

Let Jayne Ann Krentz capture your hearts with the love
stories, MAN WITH A PAST and TRUE COLORS.

And in October, watch for the second two-in-one
collection by Barbara Delinsky!

Available wherever Harlequin books are sold.

Have You Ever Wondered If You Could Write A Harlequin Novel?

Here's great news—Harlequin is offering a series of cassette tapes to help you do just that. Written by Harlequin editors, these tapes give practical advice on how to make your characters—and your story— come alive. There's a tape for each contemporary romance series Harlequin publishes.

Mail order only

All sales final

✂ ---

Clip this coupon and return to:

HARLEQUIN READER SERVICE
Audiocassette Tape Offer
3010 Walden Ave.
P.O. Box 1396
Buffalo, NY 14269-1396

I enclose my check/money order payable to HARLEQUIN READER SERVICE for $5.70 ($4.95 + 75¢ for delivery) for EACH tape ordered. My total check is for $ _____ .
Please send me:

☐ Romance and Presents   ☐ Intrigue
☐ American Romance   ☐ Temptation
☐ Superromance   ☐ All five tapes ($21.95 total)

Name: _____

Address: _____ Apt: _____

City: _____ State: _____ Zip: _____

NY residents add appropriate sales tax.   AUDIO-H1D

Harlequin Superromance®

**Available in Superromance this month
#462—STARLIT PROMISE**

STARLIT PROMISE is a deeply moving story of a
woman coming to terms with her grief and gradually
opening her heart to life and love.

Author Petra Holland sets the scene beautifully, never
allowing her heroine to become mired in self-pity. It
is a story that will touch your heart and leave you
celebrating the strength of the human spirit.

**Available wherever Harlequin books
are sold.**

STARLIT-A